# The Kissing Bough

'What is this? No kissing bough? I shall rectify that tomor-row. For the meanwhile, you are in no danger of unwanted molesting from me. I am a reformed character.' Then he stopped and examined her more closely.

'Not that you do not provide temptation. You have come along very nicely, Miss Ramsey.' She looked uncomfortable, and suddenly he felt uncomfortable, too. Where had this cool lady come from? He gazed at her a moment, noticing in particular how her green eyes sparkled.

She stared back unflinchingly. 'Why do you assume no one has offered, Nick?' she asked. 'I am rather particular.'

'And so you should be. True love is worth waiting for.'

# The Kissing Bough

## Joan Smith

ROBERT HALE · LONDON

© Joan Smith 1994
First published in Great Britain 2002

This edition published by arrangement with
The Ballantine Publishing Group, a division of
Random House Inc.

ISBN 0 7090 6582 5

Robert Hale Limited
Clerkenwell House
Clerkenwell Green
London EC1R 0HT

2 4 6 8 10 9 7 5 3 1

Typeset in 11/16½pt Garamond
by Derek Doyle & Associates, Liverpool.
Printed in Great Britain by
St Edmundsbury Press Ltd, Bury St Edmunds, Suffolk.
Bound by Woolnough Bookbinding Ltd.

# The Kissing Bough

# Chapter One

'So he is finally coming home!' Mrs Lipton declared, as soon as her vestments had been removed and she and her niece were seated in the Gold Saloon at Clareview. 'I suspected as much when we received your letter, Lizzie, even before I read your invitation to spend Christmas with you.'

Lizzie, Lady Elizabeth Morgan, cast an arch glance at her other guest. 'I have his letter here,' she said. 'Perhaps you would like to glance at it, Jane.' She handed Jane the well-worn letter.

Jane Ramsey's head was the only one in the room without a cap. At twenty years, she had by no means given up hope of nabbing a husband. Neither her looks nor her fortune made it unlikely. Although she had never been called an Incomparable, the whole neighborhood agreed that she was handsome. She would happily have exchanged her Junoesque build and Titian hair for her aunt's dainty, brunette beauty. To minimize her striking size, she dressed modestly, and to tame her riotous red mane, she wore it pulled straight back from her face, secured in a bun. On this occasion she wore a sturdy gray shawl over her gown to ward off the winter drafts that inevitably invade even the best-built houses. What she could not conceal or minimize were her wide-set eyes, which were a clear, cool green.

When people first met her, they expected her to be arrogant and hot-tempered. Her size and red hair, perhaps, suggested it. They were surprised to find her not only modest, but gentle and softspoken. Having grown up in a household of women and with an invalid mama, since deceased, she had learned constraint at an early age. It was only amongst her oldest and dearest friends that her more hoydenish side was revealed.

She applied herself to the letter Lady Elizabeth had just handed her. At the first glimpse of Nick's bold penmanship, she felt a thrill seize her. Ever since the invitation to spend Christmas at Clareview had arrived, her aunt had been dropping sly hints that it was Nick's idea. Jane hastily scanned his letter now to see if it was the case. Her name leapt off the page at her.

'Let us make it a party. Invite Jane and Mrs Lipton and Pel and anyone else you can think of. I have a great surprise for you all. The warrior is home, and ready to settle down at last.'

"Invite Jane!" A smile tugged at her lips. It would be presumptuous to imagine that the surprise was what the older ladies thought, but his being ready to "settle down" did suggest it. He was going to ask her to marry him!

For three years she had been hoping for it, not without some reason. She and Nick had always been close friends. When he bought a new mount, she was the second one he called on to show it off. His best friend and her cousin, Pelham Vickers, had taken precedence. When she had put her hair up and let her skirts down and begun calling herself a young lady, Nick always stood up with her first at the local assemblies, and often repeated the honor. The three friends, Nick, Pel, and Jane, were a common sight in Amberley, the little village in Sussex where the locals purchased their necessities.

Then, just when she had reached the proper age to receive an offer, Nick had taken into his head to join the army and go off to Spain. He had always had that restless streak. Of course, he had not actually been Lord Goderich's heir at the time. Goderich's younger brother, Arthur, stood between Nick and the title. As Arthur was a widowed septuagenarian, however, it was unlikely he would either produce an heir or long survive his elder brother as the Earl of Goderich. Eventually the title and estate would fall to Nick, and he had been raised at Clareview with this possibility in mind.

Upon Arthur's death last year, Nick had become the heir presumptive. It was utterly unlikely that Lord Goderich would sire a son. He was not only bedridden, but senile. While he lived, however, Nick's right to the title was not positive. He was apparently the heir, but not the heir apparent. He did not use the title, Viscount Wyecliffe, but when he heard from Lady Elizabeth, Goderich's spinster sister and housekeeper, that Goderich had finally run completely mad and set his pillow afire, he knew it was time to come home and take up the reins of Clareview.

After Wellington's stunning victory in Spain, he was the most revered man in England. The Tory government was eager to be rid of him, and sent him to Paris as ambassador. Nick had been invited to join him there and had been sorely tempted, but he had declined. He remained in London for a few months in a liaison capacity between Wellington and the government, but now he was coming home to settle down.

'How very happy you must be, Lady Elizabeth,' Jane said, handing back the letter. 'It will be a great relief to you.'

'I couldn't be happier, my dear Jane, if they made me a duchess,' she replied, smiling from ear to ear in a way that made her look like a crocodile, for as well as protuberant eyes, she had a large mouth. There was nothing saurian about her figure, however. She was a short, roly-poly lady.

Lizzie and Mrs Lipton exchanged a smile that spoke of April and May. They had long harbored the hope of seeing Jane installed at Clareview as its mistress.

'It is time we heard the patter of little feet at Clareview,' Lizzie said.

Jane felt acutely uncomfortable. 'Nicholas has not offered for me,' she said, gently but firmly. 'Indeed, he has not written me so much as a single line since leaving three years ago, except a short note at each birthday.' How she treasured those notes. They lay in state in her desk, bound up in pink ribbon.

'But how could he?' Lizzie asked. 'It would be improper for him to write before the proposal. Not that it would have prevented him, but he knows you are much too nice to carry on a clandestine correspondence. I have kept him informed as to your doings, Jane. You may be sure of that. He always asks for you most particularly.'

Emily Lipton gave a *tsk* of playful disapproval. 'Jane is so cautious. Her papa, God bless his soul, was used to saying she would not squeal if she was stuck with a knife, but I wager she will squeal for joy when Nick pops the question.'

Mrs Lipton's appearance was in stark contrast to Lady Elizabeth's. She was extremely stylish and, at forty years, she still had enough remnants of youth and beauty to turn an elderly gentleman's head. Her chestnut hair showed just a trace of silver at the temples. Her eyes still sparkled. She had been widowed for two years. The expectation in the neighborhood was that she would not be a widow much longer.

'Really, I cannot think—' Jane said, embarrassed.

She was rapidly talked down. Without further ado, tea was called for and the older ladies began hatching wedding plans. Jane sat, half listening, making occasional demurs. She would not let herself take it for granted that Nick meant to marry her. She had thought he was coming to propose three years ago, the day he arrived at the door of the Willows wearing his new blue superfine jacket and carrying a bouquet of white roses. But he had only come to announce he had bought a cornet and was joining the army in Spain. She had stoically blinked back her tears on that occasion, and if his "great surprise" now proved to be only that he had some plans for improving Clareview, then she would blink back her tears again and admit he didn't care for her in that way.

She had had offers, and would very likely have more in the future. Her dowry of ten thousand pounds made her entirely eligible, but she did think it would be wonderful to be Nick's wife. It was not a hankering after the title, nor a wish to lord it over the local ladies as mistress of Clareview, that lured her, fine as the estate was. No, it was Nicholas Morgan, the most dashing buck in the county, whom she wanted. But then, she sternly told herself, so did all the other ladies want him. She would not moon about like a green calf if he did not offer.

How strange it would be to be mistress of Clareview. She gazed around at the grand saloon, her eyes flicking to the massive paintings by old masters, the heavy furnishings by Kent, the lovely old Persian carpets. Garlands of evergreen boughs graced the doorways and mantels in honor of the Christmas season.

11

Their perfume scented the air, calling up memories of other Christmases. And through the front windows, hung in fading golden velvet draperies with pelmetted top, she saw the park, stretching off into the distance. Capability Brown had improved it in the last century, clumping graceful groupings of trees, curving the roadway, and subduing the hills to gently rolling vistas. But he had not been able to command the weather. His fine work was often hidden by a mist from the sea, which hung damp and cold in December, here on the south coast of England.

Jane heard a sharp voice say, 'A spring wedding? Oh no, Nick will not want to wait. We can have things arranged by the end of January.' It was Lady Elizabeth speaking. 'Ask Jane what she wants.'

Jane just shook her head. 'It is too early to make plans,' she insisted.

'Well, it is not too early to change for dinner, at any rate,' Lizzie said, and stood up. 'Nick will not be here until later. He said to expect him around nine. Dear me, it has begun to snow. Ah, but that will not stop Nick. He will be here, if he has to hire a sled. Put on your best bib and tucker, miss,' she said roguishly to Jane.

Jane and Mrs Lipton went abovestairs to dress for dinner and the evening. They had been put in adjoining rooms in the east wing, away from Lord Goderich, who sometimes awoke in the night and made a racket. Lady Elizabeth's servants had unpacked and laid out their evening frocks. They both declined the offer of assistance in dressing.

Jane was happy she had had a new gown made up for the festive season. When she turned twenty, she had forsaken the pastel shades of the deb for the deeper hues of maturity, and

12

found they were attractive to her strong coloring. The dark green velvet gown was simply cut, with no excess of lace or ribbons or ruchings on the hem. The rich material clung to the curves of her body, outlining her small waist. Her only adornments were a rope of pearls and a small pair of emerald ear pendants. The gown brought out the green of her eyes, and emphasized the drama of her fiery hair. Her ivory cheeks were flushed with excitement in anticipation of the coming meeting with Nick.

Would he think she had changed much? She had been wearing her hair loose when he left. With so little experience of the world, she had felt and acted like a child. Three years of waiting, of dealing with her mama's death, and of avidly reading the news from Spain, fearing to see Nick's name in the list of casualties or deaths, had matured her. When she looked in her mirror, she saw a lady, not a girl. But deep inside that mature body and proudly held head, a little girl was still pressing her nose against the windowpane of Clareview, watching, hoping.

Dinner was an informal affair. Lady Elizabeth planned to serve a grand supper when Nicholas arrived. The table talk was all of the weather, and whether it would delay his arrival. No one was so foolish as to think it would keep him away entirely, but he might be late. They kept country hours. By seven-thirty they were back in the Gold Saloon, seated by the flaming grate, with their backs cold and their faces uncomfortably hot. They sat with their sewing or knitting in their hands; they were all sensible country ladies, and did not believe in wasting time.

The next two hours passed pleasantly. At nine-thirty they all went abovestairs to say good night to Lord Goderich. He lay in state in the grand master bedchamber, playing with a set of tin soldiers. His thinning white hair had grown long, and stuck out

13

around a nightcap. He wouldn't let anyone near him with a pair of scissors. His long, bony, bearded face and wild eyes lent him a forbidding air, but in fact, his mind had reverted to childhood. When confronted with a pretty lady, however, his body darted forward to young manhood.

'Where is my cocoa, Nanny?' he demanded when Lizzie went to his bedside.

'It is coming, Henry,' she said soothingly. 'I have brought these nice ladies up to say good night to you.'

'I'll have the redhead,' he said, with a wolfish gleam in his rheumy eyes. 'Who are you, eh?'

He asked Jane the same question every time she came.

'This is Jane Ramsey, Henry,' Lizzie reminded him.

'Robert Ramsey's lady? Nothing of the sort. She was a mouse.'

'Robert's daughter.'

'Daughter, hah! Why didn't he have the wits to have a son, like me?' Henry's one son had died of consumption at the age of six. 'Where is my son? I want my son.'

'Nick is coming home tonight,' Lizzie said, hoping this would distract the old man.

'Nick? I didn't call him Nick. I called him Ronald George. Not after that Hanoverian fool on the throne, but after my own papa. I called him Ronald for every day.' His memory came and went. It was stronger for the distant past than for more recent times.

He rambled on for a few moments, becoming excited. Lizzie led the visitors out, and they went back downstairs. The chandelier in the entrance hall was alight, casting prisms of dancing color on the marble hallway below, and the evergreen garlands that graced the gilt-framed pictures. A statue of Zeus wore a

14

garland around his neck, which only emphasized his stark nakedness. It was just as they reached the bottom step that the knocker sounded. Pillar, the butler, darted forward to answer it. Before he could reach the door, it flew open and Nicholas stepped in. Snowflakes shone like diamonds on his hat and the shoulders of his greatcoat, lending him the charmed air of unreality. He removed the hat and handed it to Pillar, then stood, just smiling at the welcoming committee, looking from face to face with an air of deep contentment.

Jane observed him closely to see how he had changed. His boyish face had altered. It was not just the complexion, darkened from Spain's sun. The deep blue eyes that used to dance with laughter had changed, too. They were graver, the whole face more manly. He looked like a soldier, that was it. Discipline had been added to his boyish charms to provide the *coup de grâce*. He was still tall and lean, but he had grown some muscles. He held himself straighter. His black hair was barbered close to his head, removing the wave that used to fall forward to enchant the ladies.

She observed all this in a second, then he was rushing forward to meet the ladies who were rushing to meet him.

'Aunt Lizzie!' He pulled her into his arms and swung her off her feet.

He spotted Jane and came forward with his hand out. He gave her hand a firm shake, and as an afterthought, leaned down to peck her cheek. It did not feel like the kiss of a lover, and her hopes shrank accordingly.

'Did you miss me?' he asked, peering down at her. She saw a sparkle of mischief in his eyes, and wondered at it. Was it the presence of his aunt and Mrs Lipton that accounted for his mild kiss?

'Welcome home, Nick,' was her discreet answer.

Mrs Lipton welcomed him, then he took a step back toward the front door. 'And now for my surprise, ladies.' His eyes danced in the old way. His lips opened to reveal a flash of white teeth. He pulled open the door and said, 'I would like you all to meet my bride, the colonel's lady, Mrs Morgan.'

# Chapter Two

To their credit, none of the ladies fainted, or even screamed. It is true that Lizzie made a strange choking sound and clutched at Mrs Lipton's gown to prevent herself from falling. Mrs Lipton turned and stared at Jane as if fearing the girl might go off into a swoon. Seeing this, Jane pitched herself forward to greet the newcomer.

'Mrs Morgan, welcome to . . . your home,' she said, feeling acutely uncomfortable. It was hardly her place to welcome the bride, but as no one else was doing it, she forced the words out. 'I am Miss Ramsey.'

'Thank you, ma'am,' the lady replied in a soft, high voice, and curtsied. It was the first time Jane had ever been called ma'am by anyone but a servant.

Nicholas turned to his bride and smiled admiringly. 'There, I told you we would surprise them.' His bride looked less than enchanted with the reaction his surprise had elicited, and Jane for one did not blame her in the least. His aunt and Mrs Lipton soon recovered from their shock and began babbling to cover their embarrassment. While coats were removed, Jane had a moment to assess the newcomer.

It did not take a genius to see why Nick had married her. If an angel came floating down to earth, it would surely resemble this lady. Her stylish bonnet was removed to reveal a halo of soft blonde curls. That sweet face, those blue eyes and long lashes, might have stepped out of a Botticelli painting. The angel had obviously visited a French modiste to acquire that striking blue silk gown. She would have been freezing in the carriage, were it not for the sable lining to her mantle. The lady's figure was less angelic. Angels did not have such full, round, high bosoms and such small waists. Her age, Jane thought, was not more than seventeen or eighteen. She was certainly in the first flush of youth.

Eventually the little throng moved to the Gold Saloon, where Nicholas was busy to arrange his bride before the grate, setting a stool in front of her to dry her dainty feet. She continued to smile shyly around without saying much.

'You must forgive us, my dear,' Lizzie said to the newcomer. 'Such a shock. We had no idea. Why did you not tell us, Nick? I would very much have enjoyed going to your wedding.'

'So you shall, Auntie,' he said merrily. 'We aren't married yet. We mean to do it up at the beginning of the New Year. I only introduced Aurelia as my bride as a little joke. You know how I like to shock you. Naturally you must all attend our wedding. Aurelia wants a lavish wedding.' His circling gaze included Jane and Mrs Lipton in the invitation.

'And what is your fiancée's last name?' Lizzie asked.

'Townsend,' Nick said. 'Aurelia is the youngest daughter of Edward Townsend.' He looked expectant, under the misapprehension that this name meant something to his listeners. 'You must have heard of him. He's famous.'

18

'The Bow Street Runner?' Mrs Lipton asked in confusion.

Nick laughed merrily. 'Good God, no. Edward Townsend is the second largest brewer in the country, after Whitbread. He is the creator of the famous Oldham Ale that has become so popular.'

'I have heard of Samuel Whitbread,' Lizzie said. 'He married Lord Grey's granddaughter. He was a friend of Charles Fox as well. Fancy a brewer's son—'

Jane saw where this was going and leapt in. 'Nick says you are the youngest daughter, Miss Aurelia. Have you many brothers and sisters?'

Miss Townsend looked her gratitude to Jane. 'I have one brother and two sisters,' she answered in a perfectly genteel voice. 'They are all married. I was visiting my oldest sister, Mrs Huddleston, in London, which is how I came to meet Nick.'

'Huddleston? Do we know any Huddlestons?' Lizzie asked Mrs Lipton. 'The name sounds familiar.'

Mrs Lipton refrained from mentioning that she was probably thinking of Sam Huddleston, the cobbler in Amberley.

'My brother-in-law used to be the MP for Manchester,' Miss Townsend explained. 'Perhaps you have seen his name in the journals. He works for Papa now, running the administration office in London.'

'Ah, an MP, that would be it,' Lizzie said, nodding, although she seldom glanced at the political news and was hardly aware they had politics in Manchester.

When Miss Aurelia's position in society had been established – a papa in brewing, but in such a large way that the aroma of hops was diluted by the sweeter scent of gold – the conversation turned to Nick's doings.

'Of course, Wellington urged me to join him in Paris,' he said, a little proudly. 'I feel myself, and told Wellington, that I think the appointment a grave error on everyone's part. The ministers fear his popularity, but they might have found something more suitable for him. To send the conqueror to France as ambassador must be a constant thorn in the side of the French. It would be as if Boney had won the war and come to England to rub salt in the wound. It would not surprise me much if Wellington is assassinated. Perhaps that is what they want.'

'Oh really, Nick!' his aunt chided.

Jane saw that his years in Spain had not brought as much discipline and wisdom as they ought. Such outspoken criticism as this might land him in the Tower.

'I know what you are thinking,' he said to his aunt, 'but as I have abandoned public life, I can say what I feel, and I feel the appointment was bad. Many agree with me, but they are too wise to say so.'

'So you are coming home to stay,' Lizzie said, gratefully latching on to this safe topic. But the joy had gone out of the homecoming for her. She could not but think Jane must be suffering agonies, and it was half her own fault. She had given Jane the notion that Nick was coming home to marry her. Of course, Jane was concealing her grief admirably. She had great countenance. As Nick's choice had been made, they must all just learn to love a brewer's daughter. At least the girl was well behaved. Quite genteel, although she hadn't much to say for herself. A pretty little thing; one could see why Nick had been bowled over by her.

Jane was certainly disappointed, but she had never allowed her hopes to soar very high. She was relieved to see that Nick had found himself a pretty and nice girl, and that they would be residing at Clareview.

Wine was served, and after some chat, Nick went abovestairs to visit his uncle. 'I shall see what sort of mood he is in before taking you up, Aurelia,' he said to his fiancée. 'He is old; his mind wanders.'

'He has got worse,' Lizzie warned him. 'He probably won't recognize you. I shall speak to Pillar about supper while you are gone. Emily,' she said to Mrs Lipton, 'perhaps you would just take a look at the table for me. It will leave the girls a moment to become acquainted.'

Jane welcomed the opportunity. Miss Aurelia had little to say in front of the group, but she felt that as Nick was marrying her, she must be something special. He had always demanded more than just a pretty face in his flirts, although a good face was certainly obligatory.

'Do you live in London with your sister?' she asked, to get the talk started.

'My home is in Manchester. Papa built a mansion there, but one cannot meet anyone interesting in Manchester.'

Jane blinked to learn that such a large city should be totally devoid of any interesting people. 'So you made your debut in London?'

'Not formally,' Miss Aurelia replied, with just a trace of annoyance. 'But Mr Huddleston knows everyone. My sister entertains two or three nights a week. And when she does not entertain, we go out. Do you like London, Miss Ramsey?'

'Oh, indeed, very much. I only visit, of course. I was not presented.'

'I wondered that such an attractive lady had not found a husband. Are there no eligible *partis* hereabouts?'

Now it was Jane who was uncomfortable. 'Until recently, I

was looking after my mama, who was ill. She died a year ago.'

'I am sorry to hear it,' Miss Aurelia said dutifully. Then she smiled conspiratorially and said, 'Don't rush into anything. You still have a few good years in you. I mean to entertain a great deal after Nick and I are married. We will spend the Season in London, of course, but he will want to be here from time to time to keep an eye on the estate.'

'I see,' Jane replied. It was not her understanding of Nick's plans, but naturally his fiancée would know.

'How did you come to meet Nick?' Jane asked a little later.

'It was the most romantic thing!' Miss Aurelia said, glowing in pleasure. 'It happened while I was shopping. I was just coming out of Miss Lanctot's – the milliner, you know. She has the best bonnets in London. I twisted my ankle, and who should be coming along to help me but Nick! He bustled me straight into his carriage and drove me home to my sister's, for I could not walk after giving my ankle such a wrench. He called Dr. Knighton – he is the Prince Regent's doctor – and stayed for dinner. Nick, I mean, not Knighton. That evening we went out dancing – and two weeks later, we were engaged. Is it not romantic, Miss Ramsey?'

'Just like a fairy tale,' Jane agreed. But she had to wonder how that wrenched ankle had recovered so quickly.

'Is there much to do hereabouts?' was Miss Aurelia's next speech.

'The riding is good, though not so comfortable in winter, of course. There is a local hunt club. We have a good circulating library.'

'That is nice. Nick tells me I must take up riding. And what about assemblies and routs?'

'Oh, that. There is a monthly assembly in Amberley.'

'Monthly! But what do you do all the other nights? I did not expect theaters or the opera in the country, but there must be private parties.'

'Yes indeed. We visit ten or twelve families.'

Miss Aurelia sighed. 'Ah well, I have my wedding plans to keep me busy.' She glanced around the room, from the fading draperies to the wellworn carpets. 'There is a deal to be done about the house as well, I see,' she added. 'I am happy that I have met you, Miss Ramsey. I daresay you are shocked that Nick is marrying me. I do not pretend to be at home in noble company. I know I have a great deal to learn, but I learn quickly. You are an older lady; you must always tell me if I am making a fool of myself.'

'I am sure you will not do that,' Jane said. She was touched at the girl's frankness, and her appeal for help, despite that reference to her being 'an older lady.' 'I expect you will find it is yourself who is looked to to set the style. You certainly put us all to the blush in matters of toilette.'

Miss Aurelia blushed. 'Thank you. I had no notion how to dress when I went to London. Marie – Mrs Huddleston – said I looked a perfect quiz in my round bonnet when I arrived at Grosvenor Square. She took me to her modiste – French, of course. I brought my finest gowns with me, so that I would do Nick proud.' She lowered her eyelids and said in her high, child-ish voice, 'I do love him very much.'

'I am sure you do.'

'Ah, here he is now,' Miss Aurelia said as he entered the room. 'Are your ears burning, sir?' she asked playfully. 'We have just been talking about you.'

'Don't believe a word Jane says,' he said, smiling fondly from one to the other. 'I wager she told you I boxed her ears when she was in short skirts, but she forgot to tell you she put a burr under my mount's saddle and nearly got me killed.'

'She did not tell me that. I see I have a great deal to learn about my *mari*. "Boxed her ears" indeed, and here I have been taking you for a gentleman.'

'A colonel and a gentleman,' he said, bowing and taking a seat beside her.

Miss Townsend dropped her playful mood. 'How is your uncle?' she asked.

'He has deteriorated sharply since I last saw him. We had a short game of soldiers. I let him beat me.'

'And his health?' she asked.

'He seems in good enough health and spirits, I am happy to say.'

As Lady Elizabeth and Mrs Lipton returned to the group at that point, Jane missed the look of disappointment that seized Aurelia's face. Lady Elizabeth herded them all in to supper.

'Doesn't this look lovely!' Miss Aurelia exclaimed. The table had been decorated with more of the evergreen garlands. Silver and crystal sparkled in the lamplight. 'You should not have gone to so much trouble, Lady Elizabeth.'

'It is not every day we get to welcome home the hero – and his bride.'

Nick seated his fiancée at his right side and they all enjoyed a hearty supper.

'Tomorrow is the day before Christmas,' Nick said, helping himself to a wedge of raised pigeon pie. 'I wrote inviting Pel to join us for a few days. I thought he might be here when we arrived.' He turned to his fiancée and said, 'You remember I told you about Pelham Vickers. Pel, for short.'

'Oh, yes, your friend. You gave him the living at St. Peter's, I think?'

'He is a sort of honorary vicar. He doesn't actually practice his calling. Shortly after I gave him the living, he inherited a fortune from a nabob uncle and hired a curate to attend to the parish.'

'A member of the squirearchy,' Miss Aurelia said. 'I look forward to meeting him.'

'I shall ask him to practice the wedding ceremony,' Nick said, gazing at his beautiful bride-to-be. 'I would like Pel to marry us.'

Miss Aurelia looked uncertain at this. Jane thought perhaps she had a relative of her own she would prefer to have perform the ceremony, but if so, she did not mention it. The conversation turned to local matters. Nick had a dozen questions to ask, and Miss Aurelia seemed eager to listen and learn.

As soon as supper was done, Nick suggested she should retire. 'I know you have been up since dawn preparing for this visit. I told you there was nothing to be frightened of. My relatives and friends have excellent taste. They all like you. When they come to know you better, they will love you as I do.' His insouciant grin peeped out. 'Well, not *exactly* as I do, but they will admire you. And now it is time for bed, miss.'

Miss Aurelia thanked her hostess very properly, said good night to everyone, and was escorted to the bottom of the stairs by Nick.

It was the first time the ladies had had a moment alone since her arrival.

'Well, what do you think of that?' Lizzie exclaimed.

'She seems very nice. Pretty,' Jane said.

'A brewer's daughter!' Lizzie said.

Emily Lipton shook her head sadly. 'If Jane can live with it, then I don't see that you and I have anything to complain of, Lizzie,' she said.

'It could be worse,' Lizzie said, trying to accept it. 'She must be rich as Croesus. A dot of twenty-five thousand at least, I should think. Whitbread is a millionaire, and if Townsend is the second largest brewer in the country, he must be high in the stirrups. I am surprised Nick had the sense – not that I mean to say he is marrying her for her money. He is not that sensible, unless he has changed a great deal. It is odd she did not bring a woman with her, is it not? They must have been traveling since dawn.'

'They are engaged,' Jane pointed out. 'And it is not as though they spent a night at an inn.'

'Still, a *lady* would have had a companion,' Lizzie said. 'What if they had been caught overnight in the snowstorm? It is in those little details that breeding tells. We must see that she behaves herself.'

Jane, remembering her private conversation with the girl, said, 'She will. She is eager to learn. I think she and Nick will suit very well.'

That was the position she had taken, and she meant to stick by it. When Nick returned to the table, they all expressed their satisfaction with his bride-to-be. He had expected a little more enthusiasm, and mentioned what he called her 'fabulous beauty.'

'Beauty is only skin-deep,' Lizzie said, rather curtly. 'I think you are rushing into things, Nick, marrying a stranger. There are ladies closer to home whose character is well known to us all.' Her eyes slid to Jane as she spoke. 'But that is your concern. For your sake, I am sure I wish you both happy. And now I shall retire.'

She patted Jane's shoulder in a consoling manner as she left the table. Nick noticed it, and wondered about that 'ladies closer to home.' Was it Jane she was referring to? Surely she didn't think there was anything between Jane and himself? What nonsense! Why, Jane was the first one to welcome Aurelia.

Mrs Lipton soon rose as well. 'You won't be long, Jane,' she said, before leaving.

'I shall be up right away,' Jane assured her. She and Nick followed Mrs Lipton from the dining room and stopped at the bottom of the staircase.

'Well, what do you think of her, Jane?' he asked. 'I value your opinion.'

'She is exceedingly beautiful. She is friendly, nice. I like her.'

'Did you ever see such eyes? They put sapphires to shame. And that hair, like spun gold. I mean to have her portrait painted by Sir Thomas Lawrence as a belated wedding gift to myself. He is the foremost portrait painter in the country. And he is a particular master of the romantic style, which will just suit Aurelia. She wants to have me painted in my scarlet regimentals as a companion piece. I hope Sir Thomas will agree to come to Clareview to do it.'

'If not, you could have it done in London in the spring,' Jane suggested.

'Oh, I should not like to waste my time sitting for a portrait for the few days we will be in London then. Aurelia will want to go up for a ball or two, but spring is the busiest time about the estate. And so pretty, too, with the fruit trees in bloom. I mean to settle down and enjoy the simple pleasures of rural life. I have had my fill of excitement.' A shadow of memory darkened his eyes. Jane wondered what he was remembering – some battle, from the way his lips firmed so grimly.

'I am sure something can be arranged. And now I must go up, before Aunt Emily takes the notion—' She came to an embarrassed stop.

'The notion that I am trying to nudge you under the kissing bough?' he asked, smiling. He looked to the archway into the saloon, where the mistletoe usually hung. 'What is this? No kissing bough? I shall rectify that tomorrow. For the meanwhile, you are in no danger of unwanted molesting from me. I am a reformed character.' Then he stopped and examined her more closely.

'Not that you do not provide temptation. You have come along very nicely, Miss Ramsey. What ails the gentlemen hereabouts that none of them have offered for you? Slow tops!'

He sensed a new reserve in Jane when this subject of his romantic waywardness arose. She looked uncomfortable, and suddenly he felt uncomfortable, too. He was accustomed to thinking of Jane Ramsey, when he thought of her at all, as a hoydenish teenager with flying red hair and freckles. Where had this cool lady come from? He gazed at her a moment, noticing in particular how her green eyes sparkled.

She stared back unflinchingly. 'Why do you assume no one has offered, Nick?' she asked. 'I have refused a few offers. I am rather particular.'

'And so you should be. I suggest you hold out until the right one comes along, as I did. True love is worth waiting for. It hits you like a thunderbolt. And now I shall let you go. Good night.'

He placed a chaste kiss on her cheek, and watched as she walked slowly upstairs. Her velvet gown shimmered as she swayed gracefully. He admired her, in a purely aesthetic way. Yes, Jane really deserved someone special.

A vague sense of unease accompanied Jane to bed. Nick spoke of settling into his role of country gentleman, but she thought that Miss Aurelia had other plans. She wanted to cut a dash in London society. It was odd, too, about the miraculous recovery of her wrenched ankle. Was it possible that Miss Aurelia had exaggerated her injury to get Nick to accompany her home? Well, what if she had? It would not be the first time a lady had taken maximum advantage of a situation to catch a gentleman's interest.

In any case, there was no doubt that Nick was well and thoroughly fascinated by her. He could hardly stop raving about her eyes and hair. He hadn't said much about her personality, though, or her character. And he spoke of getting married early in the New Year, when he had only known her for two weeks. But basically Miss Aurelia seemed like a nice girl, even if she did call her ma'am. She was young; if she had faults, they could be corrected. Nobody was perfect.

What bothered her more was Nick's kiss on the cheek. If that was not a thunderbolt that had struck her, it was something very like it. Her cheek still tingled from his touch.

# Chapter Three

*M*any a night in Spain, while bivouacking on hard ground, or in a haystack, or in the shadow of a cannon, Nick had dreamed of being home, sleeping safely on his own feather tick again, with a cloud-soft goosedown pillow beneath his head. He was thus disappointed that his first night's slumber at Clareview was so restless. It was the visit to his uncle, playing at war with the tin soldiers, that caused it. He had a nightmare about the bloody battle of Badajoz, where his best friend, Colonel McMaster, had been killed, and Nick was promoted to colonel on the field of battle to take his place. The thunder of the guns, the heat and dust and blood, came back to him with a vividness that shook him to the core.

What a relief to lie peacefully in a quiet room and listen to the soft creaking and cracking of timbers. He gazed out the window as the first light of dawn crimsoned the sky, to watch the sun rise on a world blanketed in snow. No footprints or carriage wheels marred the pristine surface, stretching white down through the park, and off into the distance. He watched the stars fade as the sky lightened from an inky blue to clear azure, with a blinding sun that turned the snow to diamonds.

God, but he was glad to be home. By next Christmas, he would have a son in the nursery, if all went well. Life was too uncertain; a man had to take care of the necessities while he could. He knew his family thought he was rushing things by marrying Aurelia so soon after having met her, but dammit, a man knew when he was in love. Aurelia felt the same way, so why wait?

He heard Rufus moving quietly about in the dressing room. His batman had made it safely through the war with him. His uncle's moaning in the next room took the first sharp edge of joy from the day. One day, Nick thought, I, too, shall die in that bed – but not yet. Not until he had done something worthwhile with his life. *'Il faut cultiver mon jardin.'* That was what brought real satisfaction and happiness. He jumped from his bed in a near frenzy to get on with finding that happiness.

Within fifteen minutes he was striding down the staircase, sniffing the air for the welcome aroma of gammon and eggs, toast and coffee. He found his aunt and her female guests in the morning parlor. He greeted them all warmly, but Jane noticed he did not single her out in any manner.

After they had exchanged greetings, he said, 'Aurelia will sleep late this morning. She was up at the crack of dawn yesterday. We had a hard day's driving, but she is a game chick. She never uttered a complaint. Is there anything I can do to help with the preparations for Christmas, Aunt Lizzie?'

'Cook has the preparations in order for dinner. She has made her plum pudding and mince pies. She has ordered the crabs for roasting.'

'The mummers will be calling as usual, I hope?'

'I expect so. They came last year.'

'Good. Good. I mean to take Aurelia calling on the tenant farmers today. They will want to meet her. Shall I take the Christmas blankets or—'

'Most of them are already delivered, as the cold set in so early this year. I am making up a special box for Mrs Dooby. She had twins this time, poor woman. That makes nine children.'

'Poor woman?' he asked. 'Why, she is blessed nine times. Were they boys or girls?'

'Both boys. As like as peas in a pod, they say.'

'Boys,' he said, shaking his head in jealous wonder. 'We shall have to move her to a larger house.'

'The houses are all occupied, Nick,' his aunt said. 'Fogarty makes sure of that.' Fogarty was Lord Goderich's agent.

'Then we must add a room to Dooby's present house. Boys need space to grow. You have done an excellent job of preparing for Christmas, Auntie, but there is one little thing you have forgotten.'

'The spiced punch,' she said, nodding. 'I have not forgotten. We always make it up late in the afternoon, so it will not all be drunk before the mummers come. Now, there is something you could do. Mind you go light on the wine. The mummers stop at a dozen houses. We don't want them staggering home.'

Nick gave a rueful grin. 'That is a reference to the year Pel and I added brandy instead of wine and caused a scandal in the parish. I shall adhere to the family receipt. I have become a traditionalist. I shall teach Aurelia how to make it. That is the sort of thing I missed when I was away – the traditions, the rituals. Roast beef and plum pudding on Christmas, the Maypole dances, church on Sunday. I even missed Mrs Lemmon's old piebald bonnet. I used to sit, wait-ing for it to rise up on its hind legs and neigh, when I was a lad.'

'That is naughty of you, Nick!' his aunt said, but she said it with a tolerant smile. 'That bonnet is not horsehide. It is made of white feathers over a black felt. I fancy she ran out of feathers. We all thought it quite the crack when she first wore it a decade ago.'

'I shall be sadly disappointed if she has bought herself a new bonnet for Christmas. It is strange, you know, how one disparages the traditions when one is young, and wants to "improve" everything. Now I don't want to change a single thing. Not even the chair with the jiggly leg in my dressing room, nor the watermarks on the ceiling that form the map of Africa. All I want is to have our old friends gathered around us for this happy season.' So many of his friends had died, he felt a need to assure himself that something was permanent, unchanging, in this world.

Jane saw again that shadow pass over his face, and wondered at it. She wondered, too, if his love of tradition would stand in the way of Miss Aurelia's plan to fancify the house. If she were a betting lady, she would have bet Miss Aurelia would have her way.

Nick turned to smile at her. 'Jane, Mrs Lipton – Pel, of course. It will be like old times, only better with Aurelia here to share it. Did Pel say when he would come?'

'Pelham is the hostess's nightmare,' his aunt said. 'He never replies to an invitation.'

'No, no. You have misunderstood his tactic. He doesn't reply when he plans to accept it, but he does send in a refusal.'

'He usually does show up, though often late. As he sent no reply, I expect he will come when it suits him.'

'The sooner, the better. You distracted me with your talk of punch, Auntie. What I meant you had forgotten is the kissing bough.'

34

'The kissing bush, we used to call it when I was a girl,' she said, smiling at her own memories. 'I asked the underfootman to bring in some mistletoe, but he couldn't find any, which is odd, when we have so many oak trees in the park.'

'That is an old wives' tale, that it grows on oak,' Nick said. 'I believe it had some special significance to the Druids when it grew on oak. Where we always found it was on apple trees, eh, Jane? I shall take Aurelia to the orchard. I hope Fogarty has not had it all cut away.'

Jane realized she had not quite recovered from her affection for Nick. She felt a twisting in her heart to hear him say he would take Aurelia to cut the mistletoe. She knew from experience that he would hold the bough over her head and steal a kiss. He always did that. In former times, she had been the girl under the kissing bough.

They lingered at the table for an hour, talking about old times and discussing plans for the future. The name 'Aurelia' was often spoken. Eventually the lady herself appeared at the doorway, looking refreshed and angelic, and even more beautiful after a good night's sleep. All the ladies present thought she was overdressed for a day in the country. Her blue sarcenet gown was lovely, and matched her eyes to perfection, but the sleeves stopped just below the elbow, and she wore no shawl at the rather low-cut neckline. Lizzie shivered just looking at the exposed nape of her neck.

Nick's glowing smile announced that he found her perfection. He rose and filled her plate to overflowing.

'I could not possibly eat all that!' she said, laughing.

'Eat up. We have a strenuous day ahead of us. Right after breakfast we are going to call on the tenant farmers, and introduce them to the new lady at Clareview.'

'I believe it is the custom to take them some money at Christmas, is it not? I know Papa gives his workers a little bonus. He calls it blanket money.'

'Money!' Lizzie exclaimed in horror. 'Oh, my dear, we never give *money*.'

'Here in the country, we give the actual blanket,' Nick explained.

'I shall feel like Lady Bountiful!' Miss Townsend said.

'Actually, the blankets have already been given,' he said, 'but we have one box to deliver. One of our tenants' wives has just had twins.'

'How sweet. I should love to see them.'

The lovers exchanged a melting look. Jane saw it and said, 'I must be going now. I have knitted a few things for Mrs Dooby. You can tell me where her Christmas box is, Lady Elizabeth.'

The other ladies sensed they were *de trop* and rose simultaneously, each inventing an excuse to leave the young couple alone.

As Jane left, Nick grabbed her hand and whispered, 'Thank you, dear Jane. What a thoughtful creature you are.' Then he winked, and she hurried on after the others.

There was a little commotion of finding suitably warm clothes for Miss Townsend when she was preparing to leave. Her sable-lined pelisse would keep her warm enough, even in the gig, but her kid slippers would leave her feet cold. She did not possess such an inelegant and useful item as laced boots or shoes, and utterly refused to strap on a pair of pattens. She disliked to either wear a shawl over her bonnet, or leave the bonnet at home.

'Why do we not take your closed carriage, Nick?' she asked.

'The road is not suitable. It isn't paved. I cannot risk my new carriage on that rutted lane. We have to take the gig.'

'Oh, I see. Why do you not pave the road?'

'The tenants don't have carriages, so it would be a great expense for very little reason.'

'I see,' she said, but she did not sound convinced.

'Wear my shawl, Aurelia,' Jane urged, offering the shawl off her back.

'I would like to make a good first impression on the tenants,' she said artlessly. 'They will think I am not a real lady if I come in a shawl.'

'But, my dear, you cannot go out in this frigid weather without something warm over your head,' Lady Elizabeth insisted. 'You will catch your death of cold.'

'Well, I shall wear the shawl, then. Thank you, Miss Ramsey. But I shall carry my bonnet and put it on before I go into the houses.'

Nick squeezed her chin. 'Vain creature. They will love you with or without a bonnet, as we all do.'

'I wish I had something to give the twins. Could we go into the village first, Nick?'

He drew out his watch. 'We really haven't time, my dear. We shall do it another day, and take your gift.'

Aurelia thought a moment, then said, 'I shall give each of the babies a golden guinea. I daresay that would be more welcome than a basket of fruit or some such thing, and it is not like giving money to your tenant farmers, exactly.'

The ladies agreed, after she and Nick had left, that her heart was in the right place, even if she did think that the tenants required a paved road.

'I think she is a kind little thing at heart,' Lizzie said, 'though it is rather strange – vain, really – for her to worry about making a good impression on tenants.'

'I think she wants that for Nick's sake,' Jane said. 'She wants him to be proud of her.'

'If he were any prouder of her, he would burst,' Lizzie said crossly.

They acknowledged amongst themselves once more that she would soon be the acting mistress of Clareview, and they might as well accept it. This had been thoroughly discussed and settled by the time Pelham Vickers arrived.

He came shivering into the Gold Saloon, where a fire blazed in the grate, hollering, 'Merry Christmas to all. Where is the hot punch, Aunt Lizzie? I am frozen to the marrow. What must happen but I lost a wheel, and had to wait an hour in the freezing carriage while it was repaired.'

Lady Elizabeth was, in fact, no relation to him, but from hearing Nick calling her Aunt Lizzie, he had adopted the term as well. Pelham was not a man to strike off on original paths. His papa had been a bishop, and he took holy orders, too. Although he had no real interest in the church, he liked to be called vicar.

He was of medium height and build, with a spreading stomach due to a love of ale. His brown hair seemed always either too short or too long. His philosophy was that if he got it cut short, he wouldn't have to have it cut again for a few months. He was due for a trip to the barber. His hair rested on his collar, and one wayward lock fell forward over his rosy cheeks. His teeth had a slight tendency to protrude in front, but not to a disfiguring extent. No one had ever called him Rabbit. His main charm was his good nature, which never took offense and never intentionally gave it.

'Where is Nick?' he asked, toasting his icy fingers over the fire.

'He has taken his fiancée to visit the tenants,' Lizzie said.

Pelham looked at Jane and blinked. 'Eh? You and Nick are going to be hitched? Jolly good. Congratulations and all that, but what are you doing here when you are out calling on the tenants with him?'

Jane was glad it was only Pelham who was asking this embarrassing question. 'He is marrying a Miss Aurelia Townsend, from Manchester,' she explained.

'The devil you say! Now, there is a shock for us all. Is she pretty?'

'She is extremely beautiful,' Jane said.

'Trust Nick.'

'And rich,' Lizzie added. 'Her papa is a brewer.'

'You never mean he has landed Edward Townsend's chit? By the living jingo. Townsend brews more ale than Whitbread. We will all be swimming in Oldham Ale. Townsend owns a string of tied houses as well.'

'What's that you say, Pelham?' Lizzie asked, her nose quivering in curiosity. 'He owns a good many houses?'

'Tied houses. It is what they call them when a big brewer buys a tippling house and sells only his own brew. Whitbread has a string of them as well.'

'Well!' Lizzie exclaimed, her crocodile mouth stretching in a grin. 'Nick mentioned nothing of this! Tied houses, eh? Surely that is more respectable than brewing.'

'Respectable has nothing to do with it,' Pel said. 'He is rich as Croesus. Does she have any sisters?'

'Yes, two, both married. And her brother is married as well, alas,' Jane said.

Pelham sat on the sofa beside Jane. 'Since you have lost out on Nick, p'raps you would like to marry me,' he said, unoriginal as ever. He had always assumed Nick would marry Jane; therefore, she must be an excellent catch. In his simple mind, she was filed under the category: desirable brides.

'Perhaps I would,' she replied, assuming it was a joke.

'When are they tying the knot?'

'Very soon,' Lizzie said. 'As soon as possible. How many of those tying houses does her papa have, Pelham?'

'Dozens. Perhaps hundreds by now. He is snapping them up right and left. A regular nabob.'

'I think we must have a party to introduce dear Aurelia to society,' was Lizzie's next speech. 'A ball – a New Year's Ball.'

'There isn't time to arrange a ball,' Jane said, although the notion of a party pleased her.

'A big party at least. You don't suppose she will expect us to serve her papa's ale? Dear me! I hope he won't go making Clareview into one of his tying-up houses.'

'It don't work quite like that, Aunt Lizzie,' Pelham said, and went on to explain in a disjointed fashion that the tied houses were commercial establishments.

When her head began to reel, Mrs Lipton decided it was time to change the subject. 'Nick mentioned wanting you to perform the wedding, Pelham.'

'*Me?*' he asked in astonishment, tinged with horror. 'How the devil should I know how to perform a wedding? I ain't a minister. Well, in a way, I suppose I am. I shall have George do it.' George Saintbury was his curate.

'His heart is quite set on having you do it,' Lizzie insisted. 'George will show you where to find the ceremony in the book. You have only to read it. It means a great deal to Nick. He has discovered tradition.'

'The tradition is that I pay George, and he does the work,' Pelham explained. 'He knows the *Book of Common Prayer* by heart. He can rattle off a wedding or a christening or a funeral in the twinkling of a bedpost. It is all the same to him.'

'I'll go over the ceremony with you, Pel,' Jane said, to appease Lady Elizabeth.

It did not escape her notice that Lizzie had discovered a new fondness for Miss Townsend upon learning that her papa was such a propertied gentleman. She did not fear, though, that Nick's love was based on Mr Townsend's wealth. Nick positively glowed when Aurelia was in the room. It was going to be a trying week, but she had the New Year's party to look forward to.

# Chapter Four

'Miss Aurelia goes beyond Incomparable! She is a Comparable!' was Pelham's compliment to Nicholas, after meeting the bride-to-be.

Upon the actual introduction some moments before, he had said only, 'G'day, Miss Aurelia. Happy to meet you, I'm sure. Any fiancée of Nick's—' Then Jane had given him a prod in the back, and he stopped. 'Heh heh. Not that he has many fiancées. Nor any, come to that. None at all – except yourself.'

Miss Aurelia found a curtsy beyond her, in her frozen condition, and just smiled. She had become thoroughly chilled during her trip to the tenant farms, despite the shawl and the sable-lined cape. She was placed before the blazing grate, where Lizzie courted her with a hot posset, leaving the gentlemen privacy to reestablish their interrupted friendship.

Nick was so happy to see his old friend that he ignored his foolishness and gave him a bear hug.

'And a great heiress to boot, I hear,' Pelham added, detaching himself quickly from Nick's embrace. Pel did not care for these Spanish customs.

'This is not a case of cream-pot love, my friend.'

'No, no. It is not dairies the family is famous for, but ale. Townsend's Oldham Ale. You can drink your way across England, free of charge. On the honeymoon, I mean.'

'The weather is not good for travel at this time of the year. I expect we will go up to London for a week, and make a longer trip in the spring, if Aurelia likes. But enough about me. Tell me what you are up to, Pel.'

'The same old things. Hunting, fishing, shooting. I read a book while you were away. But dash it, why waste time talking about me when you have been all the way to Spain?'

After a little conversation, they were called in to luncheon, where Lizzie soon turned the table talk in the direction of the wedding.

'Pelham is the gentleman who will be performing your wedding ceremony, Miss Aurelia,' she said. 'Or may I call you Aurelia, as you are practically family?' Aurelia smiled her permission. 'And you must call me Aunt Lizzie, like the others. Tomorrow you will see the church where the wedding will be performed. It is small, but pretty. Norman, you know.'

Aurelia's frown revealed that she was either confused or unhappy. 'Norman who?' she asked.

'Norman architecture, my dear,' Lizzie explained, without a single sign of dismay. 'The Normans who invaded England built it aeons ago. They were French, were they not, Nick?'

'Yes,' Nick said, and immediately changed the subject. He noticed Jane's surprise at Aurelia's ignorance of history, and was annoyed with Jane. 'Do you think you can handle a wedding ceremony, Pel?' he asked.

'Jane has offered to help me,' Pel replied. 'Mind you, George would do a better job of it. I would hate to make a mistake on such an important occasion and end up christening you.'

Aurelia looked helplessly from one to the other. 'But are you not a vicar, Mr Vickers?'

'I am a clergyman by profession. It is just that I am more or less retired.'

'You look very young to be retired.'

'I have been at it for years.'

'If Mr Vickers is retired, why do we not be married in London, Nick?' Aurelia suggested. 'I had thought we would be married at St. George's, in Hanover Square, where my sisters were married. Now that Mama and Papa have a set of rooms in London, my family could stay there, and yours with the Huddlestons.'

'Everyone can stay here,' Nick said. 'I look forward to our families becoming friends. They must come a week before the wedding and make a little holiday of it.'

'But they always like to take their holiday in London. There is so much to do there.'

'There will be plenty to do here, Aurelia,' Lizzie said. 'We are going to have a great party to introduce you to everyone. And then the wedding a day or two later, whatever you like.'

'A ball?' Aurelia said, consideringly.

'There is not time for a proper ball. Just a party.'

Aurelia had her little heart quite set on a wedding at St. George's. On the other hand, Clareview was a rich and famous estate, and her family would enjoy seeing it. She had planned to fix it all up before inviting them. The carpets were downright tatty, and the window hangings were faded. Marie would be shocked at their condition. She had bought everything brand-new when she married Mr Huddleston. 'Do you think we could have the house ready in time?' she asked.

'We shall set the servants to work with beeswax and turpentine,' Lizzie replied. 'Have the carpets beaten, or perhaps a good brushing with tea leaves, as the weather is so inclement.'

'That sounds lovely,' Aurelia said in her whispery voice. With five pairs of eyes studying her, she had not the courage to object. She would talk to Nick privately later and explain to him that she wanted to be married in London. Meanwhile, the party sounded exciting.

'This afternoon we are going out to cut the mistletoe,' Nick said to her. 'For the kissing bough, you know.'

'You grow it yourself?' Aurelia asked in amazement. 'At home, a man used to come to the door selling it. It was convenient, in such chilly weather.'

'We cut our own,' Nick said. 'If you have never seen it growing, you will be interested to see it is a parasite. It grows on other trees, usually apple trees.'

'A parasite!' she exclaimed. 'I thought a parasite was a person.'

'P'raps you are thinking of a pharisee,' Pelham said.

'I don't think so. Papa used to call Cousin Edward a parasite. He comes and stays with us for months at a time without ever offering to pay a penny.'

Miss Aurelia found the gentlemen's talk so difficult that she turned to Jane, engaged her in more rational discourse about the shops in Amberley, and enjoyed the rest of the meal.

She was really not looking forward to another bout of the cold weather, but as soon as lunch was over, Nick said, 'Shall we go and cut the mistletoe now, my dear?'

Aurelia looked longingly at the grate, and thought of the fashion magazines in her room. She wanted to curl up in front of the fire and pore over the pictures, choosing gowns and suits and bonnets for her future life as mistress of Clareview, and eventually, as Lady Goderich.

'It is very cold out,' she said. 'It was not snowing when we left London. I did not bring any stout shoes with me.'

'You must wear mine,' Jane offered at once, and was rewarded with a testy look.

'I have already been out once today,' Aurelia said. 'Why do you not go with Nick to cut the mistletoe, Miss Ramsey?'

Jane looked at her in perplexity. She did not want to make a mountain of the little matter. It was perfectly clear that Aurelia did not want to go, and equally clear that Nick wanted her to.

'We'll all go, like in the old days,' Pelham said. 'Nick, me, and Jane. Let the girl stay by the fire, Nick. You have frozen her once today. You don't want her to come down with the flu so close to the wedding.'

This warning brought Nick's urgings to an immediate halt. 'I am a selfish beast,' he declared. 'Wrap yourself up warmly and stay in front of the fire, my dear, and have a nice hot cup of tea waiting for us. We shan't be long.'

He accompanied her to the sofa and wrapped her in a shawl. Before leaving, he placed a light kiss on top of her head. Aurelia looked up and smiled a sweet smile at him. She knew she could bring Nick around her thumb. He would not insist on having the wedding in some old French church in the country when St. George's was so much more fashionable. Marie had told her she must take a firm hand with him from the beginning, and she meant to do it.

The three who were going out bundled themselves up warmly, Jane in a woolen wrapper over her head and shoulders and pattens on her feet, the gentlemen in their greatcoats and boots.

Nick carried a knife to cut the mistletoe, Jane a basket to bring it home.

The snow, which had been untouched that morning, bore traces of wheels and hooves and human footprints now, but as they wended their way back to the orchard, they encountered virgin snow again. Jane noticed the strange smile Nick wore as he looked all around at it.

'It is a long time since you have seen snow, I expect?' she said.

'Yes, it is quite a novelty for me. I should not have urged Aurelia to come with us. I wish you will tell me when I am being unconscionably selfish, Jane.'

'I told you,' Pel reminded him. 'It was clear as a pikestaff Miss Aurelia didn't want to come out. Why would she, on a day like this? What you ought to do is go home and sit with her. Jane and I can cut the mistletoe.'

'No, no. I have been looking forward to it,' he insisted.

They entered the orchard, where an inch of newly fallen snow sat on the branches like icing on a cake. On two or three trees, clumps of mistletoe hung heavy with their burden of snow. Jane reached up to brush the snow away.

'This one,' she said. 'It has plenty of berries.' Nick cut it off, and placed it in her basket.

They selected other branches until the basket was full.

'We are forgetting something,' Pelham said. Jane had noticed the outing was less enjoyable than other years, and knew the reason was curled up before the grate in the Gold Saloon. 'What is that?' she asked.

He held a branch over her head and kissed her. 'That is what the kissing bough is all about, eh?'

She gave an uneasy laugh, wondering if Nick would also

perform the ritual. He just looked on, smiling, then took the bough from Pelham and added it to the basket.

'Let me carry that, Jane,' he said, taking it from her.

They returned to Clareview, talking about other Christmases. This is probably the last time I will be coming here with Nick, Jane thought. Once he is married, and Aurelia's family come for Christmas, they won't want me underfoot. Probably Aunt Emily and I will come for Christmas dinner, but we won't be cutting the mistletoe or sharing these little outings, which have always been a part of my life. I shall have to find new traditions.

When they returned, there was no one in the saloon. The butler told them Miss Aurelia had gone abovestairs to write letters, and the other ladies had retired to Lady Elizabeth's parlor. As Jane's feet were cold and wet, she went abovestairs to change her stockings.

Miss Townsend's head peeped out the door of her room. 'Oh, you are back,' she said. 'Is Nick downstairs?'

'Yes, he and Pelham are going to hang the mistletoe.'

'Was Nick angry that I didn't go with him?'

'Not at all.'

'It is so cold out,' she said, shivering. 'I noticed at breakfast that Lady – Aunt Lizzie gave me some strange looks when I mentioned giving money to the tenant farmers. And at lunch, too, I fear I made a fool of myself. I have always lived in the city, Miss Ramsey. I don't understand country ways yet, but I want to learn. I hope you will tell me if I am doing something wrong. I feel so ... strange here, amongst all these people who have known each other forever. I hope you will be my friend.'

Jane was touched at this artless speech. Since her best friend's marriage and remove to Kent, she had no really close lady friend her own age. It seemed natural and right that Nick's bride should become her new friend. She might prove useful to Aurelia in small ways, as she was a little older, and familiar with life at Clareview.

'I should like it of all things,' she said.

'May I call you Jane, then? And you must call me Aurelia.'

'I have been, finding "Miss Aurelia" quite a mouthful,' Jane said, smiling.

She followed Jane into her room and sat on the bed while Jane changed her stockings. 'Nick is very handsome, is he not?' she said, peeking into the mirror and patting her curls. 'Even if he weren't going to be a lord, I would still have accepted him. Marie says it is vulgar to be chasing after a title, but I think she is just jealous because Mr Huddleston has none.'

'Actually, Nick doesn't have a title yet, so no one can accuse you of that.'

'But he will have, as soon as his uncle dies.'

'Yes, it is pretty sure Nick will be Lord Goderich one day.'

'It is very exciting about the party, is it not?'

'Indeed it is. We don't have many parties hereabouts.'

'When I am Lady Goderich, I shall have a grand ball every season. And I shall find a *parti* for you, too, Jane. And now I must go to Nick.'

She bounced off the bed and darted from the room, leaving Jane behind to finish her toilette. Jane was happy that Aurelia wanted to be her friend. She had some vague image of herself as Aunt Jane, dandling the future heir to Clareview on her knee.

As she returned below, she saw from midway down the great circular staircase that the mistletoe had been hung in the archway into the Gold Saloon. Beneath it, Nick and Aurelia stood, embracing. His black head was suspended over her glinting blonde curls. What a pretty, romantic picture they made! Jane was ambushed by a jolt of anger that made her forget all her good intentions of becoming Aurelia's mentor. She had to clench her lips to fight down the wild surge of jealousy.

No, surely not jealousy! Envy – that diffused emotion, not centering on personalities but on the fact that Aurelia was engaged and she was not – was more acceptable to her. She was just a little envious. What lady would not be? She hesitated a moment, not wanting to interrupt them. Then Nick's head rose, he said something to Aurelia, they walked back into the saloon, arm in arm, and Jane arranged her face into a smile to join them.

# Chapter Five

'You tell him, Jane,' Aurelia said when Jane joined Nick and his fiancée in front of the grate. Pelham was there as well, reading, which was an unusual occupation for him. Jane chose the chair beside Pelham.

'Tell him what?' Jane asked.

'Tell Nick he must wear his scarlet regimentals tonight. Lady Elizabeth has invited some friends in for dinner. The mummers will be coming later. I want him to wear his uniform.'

'And I never want to see it again,' Nick insisted.

'You promised you would have your portrait painted for me in your uniform.'

'I would like to see you in your uniform,' Jane said. 'I should think all the neighbors expect to see you wearing it at least once.'

'I am no longer an officer. I have resigned my commission,' Nick insisted.

'Wouldn't mind seeing it myself,' Pel said. 'Mean to say, been hearing of your heroics forever. I'd like to see the shako and gold braid and all. Really ought to wear them once. A kind of a duty, in a way.'

Aurelia adopted a moue and said, 'Please, Nick. For me.'

'Tell you what,' Pel said. 'Wear 'em to church tomorrow, let the whole town gape at 'em, then put 'em away in mothballs. You'll never hear the end of it until folks get a look at you in the outfit.'

Nick looked around at the three demanding faces, from Aurelia, to Pelham, to Jane. Then he gave a reluctant *tsk* and said, 'Very well, one last time at church tomorrow, then they go into mothballs.'

'Until we go to London to have our portraits done,' Aurelia said, and laughed, pleased that she had partially won her way. She could not leave well enough alone, and added, 'Since the outfit will be all pressed and ready, perhaps you will wear it for the New Year's ball, too, to let my family and friends see it.'

He gave a look of mock intimidation. 'There are limits to my patience, my little turtledove. And the New Year's do is not to be a ball, but an informal rout.'

Lady Elizabeth and Mrs Lipton joined them and approved of the idea of Nick wearing the uniform to church for Christmas.

'Be sure you stop in to show it off to your uncle,' Lady Elizabeth said. 'Have you been in to see him today, Nick?'

'Certainly I have, and will go again. Is he awake now?'

'Yes, he was asking for you.'

'Let us go up, then,' he said to Aurelia, and they left.

'What a dear child she is,' Lady Elizabeth said. Her crocodilian smile coerced them all to agree.

Jane said to Pelham, 'Is that the wedding ceremony you are studying, Pel?'

'Eh? What would a wedding ceremony be doing in a cookery book? I am looking at the receipt for mulled wine. Port or claret, it says. Which do we use?'

'We used claret last year.'

'So we did. It don't mention the apples. We always have apples floating in the wine. Do you have any apples in the root cellar, Aunt Lizzie?'

'Of course we have apples. And don't forget to use the proper tin warmer for the wine. Mulled wine requires its own special pan.'

Jane studied Pelham as they worked together. She was reluctant to give up the past. If she married Pel, things would continue on much as they always had. True, she didn't love him, but she liked him very much. He would make a good, thoughtful husband. There was no one she liked better – except Nick, of course, and as he was marrying, why should not she?

While the preparations for the mulled wine were taking place in the saloon, abovestairs Lord Goderich surveyed the two young strangers who had come into his room. Then he recognized Nick and demanded to know who the young chit with him was.

'This is Miss Aurelia Townsend, uncle, my fiancée.'

'I thought you was marrying that Junoesque redhead that was in here last night. Rob Ramsey's gel, is she?'

'Indeed she is, but my fiancée is Miss Aurelia.' He said aside to Aurelia, 'Say something to him.'

Aurelia stepped closer to the frightening old man on the bed, who looked like a bedlamite with his white hair flying about and his wild eyes staring at her. Words stuck in her throat. What on earth did one say to a lunatic lord? In society, she was invariably introduced as the youngest daughter of Edward Townsend, the brewer.

She curtsied and said timidly, 'I am Aurelia, Edward Townsend's daughter, sir.'

'Eh? Who the deuce is Edward Townsend? There are no Townsends hereabouts.'

'Papa is a brewer,' she said.

'Ah, a brewer! Excellent. Bring me a glass of ale, miss.' Mistaking her for a serving wench, despite her elegant gown, he reached out his fevered finger and pinched her chin.

She emitted a frightened squeak and jumped back. 'Let us go, Nick,' she said. 'He *touched* me!' Nick looked unhappily surprised at her reaction.

'Ha ha! I'd like to do more than touch you, saucy wench!' Lord Goderich cackled. 'Come here and give me a kiss.'

Aurelia said, 'Ohhh!' in horrified accents, and fled from the room.

'Now, Uncle, behave yourself,' Nick said, laughing in spite of himself. 'Miss Aurelia is my girl.'

'And a mighty tasty morsel she is, too. Is she good in bed?'

'Time will tell.'

'You don't want to let Ramsey's gel get wind of what you are up to, lad. Mistresses are fine in their place, but you shouldn't have brought her here. Don't sow your wild oats in the home paddock.'

Nick saw there was no point repeating that Aurelia was his fiancée. Rational conversation was so difficult that he said, 'Are you on for a battle, Uncle?'

'Get the soldiers,' was Goderich's reply.

Nicholas arranged the soldiers on the counterpane and they engaged in a short battle. When it was over, he put his arms around his uncle and hugged him. He was astonished at how fiercely his uncle returned the pressure. When he stood back, there were tears in the old man's eyes.

'That felt good,' he said. 'A man needs a human touch from time to time, even an old relic like myself. I miss my good lady. I do.'

'I'll come to tuck you in tonight.'

'You do that. You're a good lad, Ronnie.' Ronald was Lord Goderich's son, who had died so young. Goderich had been like a father to Nick, and he was pleased that his presence could bring some pleasure to the old man in his last days. He remembered his uncle as a vibrant man, riding to hounds, or sitting at the head of his table, at other times receiving callers in his study. The most important man in the parish – and now he had come to this pathetic figure, begging for a human touch. Nick was in a pensive mood when he joined Aurelia, who had waited all the time in the corridor.

'I don't want to go in there anymore, Nick,' she said. 'That old man frightens me.'

'He frightens me, too,' Nick said. 'I don't like these reminders of mortality.'

They went, hand in hand, to the staircase. Nick clung to her as his uncle had clung to him, as if holding on to life.

'Then we won't have to see him again?' she asked.

A sharp rebuke rose in his throat, but he quelled it down. It wasn't Aurelia he was angry with, but life, or more accurately, death. Goderich could mean nothing to her.

He said, 'Naturally I must visit him. He is my uncle – for all practical purposes, my father. There is no need for you to see him, if it displeases you.' But he thought it would be nice if she could have put up with the old man, for his sake.

'He called me a wench!'

'He called me Ronald.'

'There you are, then. He doesn't even recognize you. He cannot leave the estate and title to anyone else, can he? Marie said it was entailed.'

'No, he can't.'

Aurelia noticed that Nick was unhappy, and naturally assumed that she was the cause. To atone for whatever she had done wrong, she said, 'You should let him see you in your regimentals, Nick. I wager he would like that.'

'So he would. I shall be sure to visit him in full regalia.'

Pelham had drawn a table up in front of the grate when they went below. He and Jane were gathering the ingredients for the mulled wine, which would be made over the grate after dinner. Jane looked up when Nick and Aurelia entered, and knew at once that something was bothering Nick. His eyes wore that shadowed look again.

'How is your uncle? Not worse, I hope?' she asked.

'About the same. I must visit him more often. He is lonesome up there.'

'Shall I go up now? I could take some cards, or read to him for an hour before dinner.'

'You don't mind? He might—'

'Pinch my bottom?' she asked, and laughed. 'He has tried that before now. I can keep him in line, never fear.' Then she frowned. 'Though I hate doing it, somehow. I remember him as he was in the old days, so powerful. Almost forbidding.'

Nick gazed at her a moment, with a pained look in his eyes. 'Yes, I was just thinking something like that myself.' He took her hands in his and said, 'It would be a kindness if you would visit him, Jane.'

'I shall go at once.'

When Nick went up to change for dinner an hour later, he

heard laughter coming from his uncle's room, and went to investigate. Jane had pulled a chair up to the bedside and was playing a simple card game of all fours with Goderich.

'My point!' Goderich exclaimed, and, cackled in glee.

She tapped his hand playfully. 'Cheat! You know perfectly well that was my ace!'

'Heh heh. I win! Game over. You must pay the forfeit!' Goderich looked up when Nick entered. 'Ah, here is Nick!' he exclaimed.

Nick noticed that his uncle was smiling. Even his eyes looked a little brighter – and he had not mistaken him for Ronald.

'Pay up, miss!' Nick said, stepping in.

'You don't deserve it. I know perfectly well you cheated,' Jane scolded, but she placed a quick kiss on the old man's cheek.

'It is time to dress for dinner, Jane,' Nick said.

'You've come to steal my girl away, eh?' Goderich said archly. 'Can't say I blame you. She is a prime and plummy chick.' Then he turned to Jane. 'If you promise to come back tomorrow, I'll let you win,' he said.

'I see what you are up to, sly dog!' Nick chided. 'You just want an excuse to kiss Jane.'

'And who shall blame me?' Goderich responded. 'She is a fine-looking woman. Mighty fine.'

Jane rose and curtsied. 'Thank you, kind sir. Now I must eat. And so must you. Your sister tells me you have not been eating properly.'

'Scold, scold, scold! You ladies are all alike,' Goderich said, but he looked pleased with the attention.

'This is very kind of you,' Nick said as he accompanied Jane to her room. 'Uncle looks better already, after your visit.'

'We found visits helped with my grandpapa, when he was ill in bed for so long. The doctor said the stimulation of company was good for him. It keeps the mind active, you know. It will be even better, having you home, Nick. What a shame he will not be able to attend your wedding.'

'I fear the church is beyond him, but I have not given up hope entirely.'

'You must take Aurelia in to visit him, in her wedding gown, at least.'

'Yes. A pity she is frightened of Uncle. Or perhaps disgusted with his senility. He does look odd with his hair so long, and that beard.'

'She is young. She will get used to his ways, in time. She is very sweet, and eager to please you. Could you not convince your uncle to have his hair cut, and a shave?'

Nick smiled at her in a conning way. 'I wonder if a pretty young lady would not have more success in that line? I wager you could tease him into it.'

They had reached her door. She curtsied and said, 'I shall try my poor best.'

A pretty flush suffused Jane's cheeks at Nick's intimation that he found her attractive. In the shadowed hallway, her Titian curls looked nearly black, forming a dramatic contrast to her ivory skin. He realized that, as his uncle had deteriorated, Jane had blossomed from a pretty young hoyden into a beautiful, poised woman. What a wonderful wife she was going to make for some fortunate gentleman.

He leaned against the doorjamb and said, 'Are you seeing anyone, Jane?'

She looked startled at the question. 'A beau, do you mean?'

'Yes. Is it not high time you were choosing your husband?'

'Strange you should ask. As a matter of fact, I had an offer just today.'

'Today! But, you haven't seen anyone.'

'*Au contraire*! I have seen Pelham.'

'Pelham!' he exclaimed, detaching himself from the doorjamb to stare at her. 'Good God, you can't be serious.'

'Why not? He is eligible. I have known him forever, and like him very much. He is only a distant cousin, if that.'

'But you can't love him!'

'Well,' she said consideringly, 'I don't exactly love him, but I think I might try. As you said, it is time I choose a husband, and they are in rather short supply hereabouts. When he kissed me—'

Nick's eyebrows rose in surprise. 'Kissed you? It has reached that stage, has it? Stealing kisses behind doors.'

'No, under the kissing bough.'

'That was only a peck on the cheek. Have there been more . . . shall we say, ardent embraces?' He watched as a light flush rose up her throat to color her cheeks. He could not remember ever having seen Jane blush before. Damme, if she hadn't gone and grown up on him. And done a fine job of it, too. He found himself wondering what it would be like to kiss Jane Ramsey. A tingling along his veins cautioned him of the impropriety of his thoughts.

'Nothing that caused an assault of thunderbolts,' she admitted.

'Then you don't love him. You have only decided it is time to marry. Pel is not the man for you. He—'

She gave him a very knowing look. 'He is not only my cousin, but your best friend, Nick. I hope you aren't going to say something horrid. I know he is a bit awkward, but he has a heart of gold. Looks are not so important to a lady as they seem to be to a gentleman.'

Nick just stared. She was serious! It was the most ludicrous thing he had ever heard, to think of Jane marrying Pelham. He wiped his hand across his mouth, as if to wipe away the words that wanted to come out.

'Well, if that don't beat the Dutch!' he said, and strode angrily away. What did she mean by that crack about looks being so important to a gentleman? Was she implying some lack in Aurelia? Aurelia was only eighteen. What did she expect? The savoir-faire of a dowager?

Jane's heart was pounding when she closed her door and lit the lamp. What a strange reaction! She had thought Nick would be happy at her choice. The old circle of friends complete again, enlarged by the addition of Nick's wife. They could have wonderful times together. But Nick was definitely not pleased – and he hadn't even the grace to let on he was. She was bending over backwards to be nice to Aurelia. Why could he not say something nice about his best friend?

# Chapter Six

Nick saw no evidence, that evening, of Jane Ramsey and Pel being anything but the good friends they had always been. The family party was enlarged by a dozen neighbors who had been invited for dinner, but that need not have prevented the couple from displaying some tokens of affection. He had only an occasional moment to consider the shocking thing Jane had told him. He was kept busy greeting guests and accepting their compliments on his military career, his return to Clareview, and of course, his betrothal.

Aurelia had a tendency to freeze into silence when presented with a crowd of strangers, so that he had to stay close to her and occasionally smooth her conversational path. His neighbors beamed on her, apparently well pleased with his choice. If there were a few more jokes about Oldham Ale than he would have liked, he was careful not to reveal it.

Old Lady Bingham got him aside and said conspiratorially, 'Your young gel is nothing to be ashamed of, Nick. Lizzie will show her how to go on in society. Half the aristocracy are snapping up these rich merchants' daughters. It seems to me you have got the best of the lot. Oldham's daughter! What size of dot is he giving her?'

'We have not discussed details yet, ma'am,' he replied stiffly. 'I am not marrying a dowry, but a lady.'

'That's it! Mount up on your high horse and stare them all down. But just between ourselves – how much?'

'Enough,' he said, as Lady Bingham was a good friend of his aunt's, and he could not like to insult her.

He heard whispers of forty or fifty thousand, which was ludicrous. Townsend had four children. Presumably the bulk of the fortune would go to his son. He had only met Mr Townsend once, for a brief visit. He had not offered for Aurelia at the time. It was Marie who had given her consent to the marriage. She had told him her papa had given herself, the eldest daughter, twenty thousand, the second daughter fifteen, and Aurelia was to get ten, which was certainly not sufficient to 'buy' him, if he were for sale. The ten thousand, however, appeared to be a flexible sum, capable of doubling if it should be necessary.

Immediately after dinner, Nick and Pelham joined Jane and Aurelia at the grate, where they were beginning to prepare the mulled wine. The other guests sat around the room in groups, gossiping and getting caught up on the news.

'One cup of water for a pint of wine,' Pelham read. 'I have four quarts of wine in the pan. Toss in eight cups of water, Jane.'

'The sugar and spice have to be added to the boiling water first,' she reminded him.

'She's reached a rolling boil now,' he said, peering into the steaming pot. 'Here, let me lift the kettle off the flame and ladle it out. I don't want you to burn yourself.'

Nick looked sharp at this speech. It was the first one he had heard that held any tinge of concern for Jane. He noticed that Jane smiled fondly in appreciation. Pelham placed the boiling water on the apron of the grate.

'What spices do you use? Let me do that,' Aurelia said. 'I want to learn.'

Pelham peered at the receipt book. 'Cloves, nutmeg, and cinnamon. Here, Jane has measured them out.'

He handed her a bowl of ground cinnamon sticks and cloves, with a whole nutmeg on the side of the dish. Jane poured in the sugar, and Aurelia dumped in the spices.

Pelham frowned as the nutmeg danced around the top of the water. 'It seems to me we used to grate the nutmeg, didn't we?'

'Yes, it has to be grated,' Jane explained to Aurelia.

Pelham drew it out with a spoon and dried it off. 'Here you go,' he said, handing it back to Aurelia, who looked at it in confusion.

'What do you grate it with?' she asked.

'A grater,' Pelham replied.

Jane handed her the grater and showed her how to grate the nutmeg. Before she had been grating for a minute, she handed it to Nick.

'Here, lazybones. Your turn,' she said.

Nick knew this was exactly the sort of evening he had been wishing for. His friends were here; they were performing the old rituals together, yet he was dissatisfied. Every time Jane smiled at Pelham or spoke to him, he felt a pronounced urge to strike someone.

'Not so much sugar!' Jane exclaimed when Pel began to add a little extra.

'I like it sweet,' he said.

'You might think about the rest of us,' Nick said, rather sharply.

'Just as you like. I can always add a little to my own glass later. Here, give this a try, Jane.' Pel held the ladle to her lips. 'Careful, now. It's demmed hot.'

'A little more nutmeg, I think,' she said.

'My fingers are aching,' Nick said. 'Can't someone else take a turn?'

'Here, give it to me,' Pel said, and promptly grated the end off his finger, for the nutmeg had decreased to a minuscule size.

'I am sure you can buy nutmeg already grated in London,' Aurelia said. 'It is a great deal of work, making the mulled wine, is it not? I hope it is worth the effort.'

'Do you want a plaster for your finger?' Jane asked Pelham, taking his hand and examining the raw end of his digit.

Pelham stuck his finger in his mouth and sucked it. 'Don't believe that will be necessary, Jane. Kind of you to ask.'

'It's only a scratch, for God's sake,' Nick scoffed.

'We ain't all heroes, Nick,' Pelham said forgivingly. He nudged his friend aside for a private word. 'You seem a bit testy tonight, Nick. I know you've had a bad time of it in Spain, but you're home now. It's Christmas. You have a beautiful young fiancée. What more could you possibly want out of life? Just relax and enjoy yourself, or Miss Aurelia will think she's marrying a bear.'

'Sorry, Pel,' Nick said, and gave himself a good talking to. He was behaving like a lout. What was the matter with him? He decided it was Goderich, rapidly sinking into oblivion abovestairs, that was putting him on edge.

When the mulled wine was prepared, they all tested it and agreed it was fine.

'Forgot the apples,' Pel said, and went off in search of them.

Shortly after his return, the mummers arrived and the whole party went out to watch the performers in their painted paper costumes and flowered headgear enact the traditional Christmas performance. They were all there – King George and the Doctor and Turkey Snipe, having at each other with their wooden swords. Nick pushed his worries aside and enjoyed the show. He invited the performers in for a glass of mulled wine and cakes, then they were off to Squire Archer's house.

'Well, by jingo, that was enjoyable,' Pelham said when they had left. 'And on New Year's we will have the wassailers around to serenade us. There is nothing like a good country Christmas season.'

'Their costumes were made of paper,' Aurelia said.

'That's part of the tradition,' Pelham explained.

'Why don't they have cloth ones? At the Christmas pantomime in London they have lovely costumes.'

'That's London. This is the country,' he said simply.

Miss Aurelia thought the country had a deal to learn from London, and when she was mistress of Clareview, she would teach them the proper way to put on a show.

In the general melee after the departure of the mummers, Jane thought old Lord Goderich might enjoy a cup of the mulled wine, and took one up to him. He was allowed wine, and in fact, usually had a posset at night to help him sleep. Nick soon noticed that she was not about, and asked Pelham where she had gone.

'She took a glass of wine up to your uncle, I believe. She is always thinking of others,' he added, smiling as proudly as if Jane already belonged to him.

'I promised to visit Uncle before retiring. I had best go up now, or the wine will have put him to sleep.'

'Say good day to him for me. I stopped in earlier, but he was sawing logs.'

Jane found Goderich already asleep when she arrived, his candle guttering low in the wall sconce. She just looked at him, rather sadly. His blankets were all askew. She set the wine aside and straightened his blankets. When she looked up, Nick was standing at the door watching her, with a frown of concentration creasing his brow.

'He's asleep,' she said softly. 'Shall I blow out the candle?'

'I promised him I would come up and say good night. I hope he doesn't think I forgot.'

'He will have forgotten all about it by morning,' she said. 'We'll leave the mulled wine to let him know you were here. If he awakens in the night, it might put him back to sleep.'

'That was thoughtful of you, Jane,' he said.

'Lord Goderich was kind to me in the past. He gave me my first pony, took me on my first trip on a sailboat. I just wish I could do more for him.'

'I feel the same.'

'His time is nearly gone. You are doing what would please him – if he realized it, I mean.'

'What is that?'

'Why, you will be carrying on in his place as Lord Goderich. Marrying, running the estate, raising more sons to run Clareview. That is what he always wanted.'

'That's true, but I must confess, I came home to please myself. It never even occurred to me that it would please him. What a wise lady you are – and kind into the bargain, to cheer me up.'

She studied him a moment, wondering if it was Goderich's condition that had marred Nick's mood that evening. 'I hope I have succeeded, for you have not added much cheer to this evening's party so far,' she said frankly.

'Indeed you have.' But his smile, when they returned below, was more wistful than happy. Here was Jane, trying to repay Goderich for a few random acts of kindness, and he, who had been like a cherished son to the old man, forgot to go up and visit him when he had promised he would.

Lady Elizabeth was waiting for them when they entered the saloon. 'Are you ready now, Jane?' she asked. 'I have gathered the guests in the Music Room for some caroling.'

'You need not have waited for us,' Nick said.

'Jane is to play the pianoforte,' his aunt explained. 'My fingers are not as supple as they once were, Nick. I wrote to you about my rheumatism. Let us go along.'

'I'm sorry I kept you waiting,' Jane said, and followed Lady Elizabeth to the Music Room, where the guests stood in a semi-circle around the piano, with some of the older folks sitting a little back from the others.

Pelham came forth to greet her. 'I'll turn the pages for you,' he said.

Again Jane sensed some latent hostility in Nick, and said, 'Perhaps you would like Aurelia to play for us, Nick. Does she play the pianoforte?'

'I – I don't know,' he said, and looked embarrassed. 'You go ahead, Jane.'

Jane went to the piano and played a simple accompaniment to the old traditional carols, while the group sang. The piano was slightly out of tune; no one had played it since Lady Elizabeth's bout of rheumatism. None of the singers had a particularly well-trained or beautiful voice, yet the results were not only satisfactory but very moving. For Nicholas, it gave the profound satisfaction of a religious experience. The sensation of peace and well-being he had felt lacking all evening settled on him, and filled him with a glow of happiness.

When he glanced at the window bay, he saw snow falling softly in the blackness of night. How good it was to be home. The lamplight streaming on Jane's bent head turned her Titian tresses into a crown. No, a halo. A queen would not bow her head so modestly. Her white fingers moved delicately over the keyboard. She glanced up and saw him looking at her, and smiled softly. Yes, this was how his homecoming should be.

Lady Bingham soon glanced out the window and brought the singing to a halt.

'Good gracious, it is snowing! We had best get home or you will be saddled with us all for Christmas, Lizzie,' she exclaimed.

Others saw the snow and joined in the rush to get home. When the last guest was seen from the door, Mrs Lipton said to her hostess, 'It is time for me to retire as well. A lovely party, Lizzie. Just like old times.'

Lizzie accompanied her abovestairs, saying, 'It was. I don't like change at Christmas. When Nick was away . . .' Her voice petered out.

'Shall we polish off the mulled wine before we hit the tick?' Pelham suggested, and the others agreed.

'I hope the snow lets up, or there won't be anyone at your Christmas service tomorrow, Vicar,' Aurelia said.

'Eh? *My* service?'

'You are the vicar of St. Peter's.'

'Only the real vicar. George will tend to the service for me. He lives right next door so he will make it, whatever about anyone else. Well, how did you enjoy the party, Miss Aurelia?'

'Very nice.' Then she turned to Nick. 'If we are here for Christmas next year, I would like to give the mummers real costumes, Nick. And perhaps we could hire some singers to give us a concert afterwards. Real, professional singers, I mean.'

Nick ignored her other heretical speeches and said, 'What do you mean, *if* we are here?'

'I mean if we decide to spend Christmas here, instead of in London.'

'We always spend Christmas here,' he said simply.

'I know many folks leave London for the season, but there is really plenty to do there. The Christmas pantomime and the Christmas concerts. Marie has a big party. Mama and Papa spoke of spending next Christmas with the Huddlestons. Or they could stay with us. Your house is plenty big enough for guests.'

'But we—'

'Now, you mustn't be selfish,' she said, smiling tolerantly. 'I am spending Christmas here this year. You must let *me* choose next year.'

'Fair's fair,' Pelham said. He finished off his mulled wine and set down the glass. 'I'll see you up to your room, Jane, and let these two lovebirds have their argument in private. We are *de trop* here. That's French.'

They exchanged good nights, and Pelham took Jane's arm to lead her from the room. At the archway he stopped and pointed to the mistletoe.

'I've got you where I want you now,' he said, and placed a quick kiss on her lips. He had been aiming for her cheek, but hit her lips by accident. 'Sorry,' he mumbled, blushing.

She laughed and kissed him back on the cheek. 'What is sauce for the gander,' she said.

'Eh? I thought the saying was "what's sauce for the goose."'

'You're right. You *are* a goose. What was I thinking of?'

'It's the wine. I'm feeling a touch twisty myself.'

Nick watched them from the grate. He knew his former feeling of well-being had dissipated, and told himself it was Aurelia's suggestion of spending next Christmas in London that accounted for it. He certainly had no objection to Pel giving Jane a kiss under the kissing bough. Nothing wrong with that. He did it every year. But he didn't remember Jane ever returning the kiss before. And the way they were laughing – it had an intimate sound.

Then he looked at Aurelia. She smiled sweetly at him and held out her hand to draw him down beside her.

'We don't have to go to London next Christmas, if it makes you so unhappy,' she said.

He raised her hand to his lips and kissed it. 'I am a selfish beast. You are worlds too good for me,' he said.

# Chapter Seven

Nick made a great commotion in the household when he appeared at breakfast the next morning in his scarlet regimentals. They set off his dark coloring and broad shoulders to a tee. There were actually tears of pride in his aunt's eyes, and a mist of pleasure in his fiancée's, as they complimented him.

Nick didn't even hear Jane's breathless, 'Oh my, you do look fine!' She had often imagined Nicholas all decked out in his uniform. She found that reality outpaced even imagination. When she glanced at Pel, stolidly pushing a forkful of egg into his mouth, she felt grave doubts that she could marry him.

'Should I be saluting?' Pelham asked, not entirely in jest.

'Take a good look,' Nick said. 'The outfit goes into camphor after church.'

'No, no! Not until you have had your portrait done. You promised,' Aurelia reminded him, with an adorable moue.

A clamor soon rose in support of this notion. Jane added her voice to the others. During breakfast, there was a steady stream of servants past the door of the breakfast room, all wanting a peek at the master in his red jacket.

Nick went outdoors after breakfast to see if last night's snow-
fall had been heavy enough to make driving hazardous. He saw
sufficient snow on the ground to lend the proper festive appearance without keeping anyone home from church. It was a soft,
moist snow that clung to every bush and bough. Tracks on the
ground showed where two rabbits had passed in the night.
Black-headed coal tits rustled about the branches of the soaring
pine trees in the park, loosening snow that fell with a soft plop.

When the carriages were brought around, he saw the horses'
breath steaming into the cold air. Heated bricks had been
placed on the carriage floor to warm the ladies' feet. Fur rugs
awaited them. It had been arranged that his Aunt Lizzie and
Mrs Lipton would accompany Jane and Pelham. He had rather
hoped the four younger folks could go together, but it was
no matter. Pel could not be making up to Jane with the other
ladies in the carriage. He, on the other hand, had Aurelia to
himself.

There was no lovemaking during the trip, however. Aurelia
was concerned lest she not make a grand enough impression on
the parish.

'My bonnet is from Madame Lanctot's,' she said. 'Do you
think it pretty?' It looked like a giant steeple covered in blue
feathers and did not suit her in the least, but he didn't want to
hurt her feelings.

'It is lovely, my dear,' he said.

'I want to be the best-dressed lady in church, Nick, so you will
be proud of me.'

'My pride in you doesn't rest on bonnets,' he said, smiling at
her anxiety. 'No one will outdo you, never fear. You will quite
take the shine out of me in my uniform.'

'Oh, no! The red will stand out a mile. You look so handsome, Nick.'

'I feel like a demmed fool, but you are right. The parish will expect one look at the outfit.'

The old Norman church stood like a bastion on a hilltop, surveying the carriages and pedestrians who answered the summons of its pealing bells. The ladies of the parish had plundered their conservatories and the countryside to provide the altar with flowers and holly. For this special festival, large red velvet bows graced the ends of the pews.

Miss Aurelia caused a great sensation in the highest poke bonnet ever seen in the parish when she was led up the aisle to Goderich's box, but she took second place to Colonel Morgan. He wore not only the uniform, but the aura of a returned hero, and the next lord of Clareview. The Reverend Saintbury welcomed Colonel Morgan home, and performed the service satisfactorily. He delivered the sort of sermon expected of him on this occasion: short, with more of rejoicing at the holy season than harping on duty and sin. That would be taken care of during Lent. Mrs Lemmon's piebald bonnet nodded in approval.

Nicholas felt uncomfortable with the parish making such a fuss over him after church. He was quick to divert attention from himself by presenting Miss Aurelia, who clung to his arm, blushing prettily.

'I felt just like a princess!' was her artless comment when they finally reached the seclusion of their carriage. She behaved like one, too, waving and smiling with great condescension from the window at the crowd who peered in, eager for one last look at Nick and his bride-to-be.

'Perhaps you are right about spending Christmas here, Nick. We would not have received so much attention in London,' she said.

'I wish we had not received so much here. I am not comfortable on a pedestal. I'm afraid of falling off.'

'I like it. It makes me feel special,' she said.

The minute he was home, Nick changed into his blue jacket and buckskins. Lunch was a hasty meal, to leave the servants free to prepare the grander feast to come that night. He tried to get up a skating party for the afternoon, but had scant success. Pelham could not be pried from the grate, and Jane stayed with him. She actually wanted to go, but could not like to tag along like a third wheel with the betrothed couple.

Aurelia seemed keen for the outing. This time she did not hesitate to set aside her bonnet and bundle up warmly in shawls and mittens. She was learning to adapt to country life, and even taking some pleasure in it. Once they had left, Jane became restless. It was a beautiful day. The sun gleamed on white snow with a blinding light.

'Let us go for a short walk, Pelham,' she suggested. 'You will want to work up an appetite for dinner.'

'I find sitting by a fire gives me a good appetite,' was his reply.

'It also gives you a few extra pounds.'

'Why don't you go for a little stroll if you feel like it? I can watch you from the window.'

'Very well. You can practice the wedding ceremony while I am gone,' she said, and went to get her shawl.

She walked westward, toward the pond, but did not plan to join Nick and Aurelia. She had some deep thinking to do. Pelham's offer of marriage had been offhand, hardly an offer at all, really; but his behavior since speaking indicated a certain seriousness. She felt sure she could have him if she showed the least interest. Life as Mrs Vickers would be comfortable. Pelham was well off, well liked, and of good character, if a trifle lazy. He was not handsome, to be sure, but appearances were not really important. Like any woman, she wanted children to fill her life.

She stopped to admire the holly, with its red berries peeping through the snow. Mistle thrushes were busily stripping the berries from the bough for their Christmas dinner. They were joined by a blackbird and a flock of hedge sparrows. She saw fox tracks in the snow and followed them. They led her toward the pond. She stopped behind a stand of blackthorn bushes, not wanting Nick and Aurelia to see her. She could not say why; perhaps it was her conscience nagging at her, because every fiber of her being wanted to spy on them.

She caught a glimpse of Aurelia's blue shawl through the bushes. Strangely, she wasn't moving, but standing perfectly still. Jane peered around the bush and soon discovered the reason for it. She was in Nick's arms, being embraced very thoroughly indeed. Jane felt a painful tightening in her breast. She turned and fled back to the house. If Pelham offered for her again, she would accept.

Pelham, however, had fallen into a doze by the cozy grate. The reading material by his side was not the *Book of Common Prayer* but a hunting journal. He looked unappealing with his mouth open, emitting gentle snorts. She would cure him of these lazy habits after they were married. In the meanwhile, she went to ask Lady Elizabeth if there was anything she could do to help. Lizzie and Mrs Lipton sat in Lizzie's parlor, knitting.

'You might run up and take a look in on Goderich, if you don't mind, Jane. He was asking for you.'

'I would be happy to.'

Goderich was awake and happy to see her. 'Ronald tells me it is Christmas,' he said. Of course, he meant Nick. 'He looked gallant in his red jacket. It is good to have him home. I meant to go to church on Christmas. I think I could have made it. It don't seem like Christmas without hearing the story.'

'Why don't I read the Christmas gospel to you?'

'Ah, I would like that. Saint Luke, if you please. I could almost recite it with you. I have heard it three score and ten times. I daresay this will be the last.'

'Nonsense, you will hear it again next year, and the next.' She read the time-honored phrases. She knew them nearly by heart herself. 'At that time there went forth a decree from Caesar Augustus,' she began, and read the piece through in a clear, plain voice to the end. 'Glory to God in the highest, and peace on earth to men of good will.' She set the book aside.

When she looked up, there were tears in Goderich's eyes. He brushed them away, smiling. 'That was nice, my dear. Thank you. Ah, and who is this who has come to visit me? Your mama, I believe.'

It was Emily Lipton who had appeared at the doorway, but she did bear a strong resemblance to her sister. 'Willie Winston has just arrived, Jane,' she said. 'I spotted him at church this morning. He was asking for you. If you want to go down and say hello, I shall sit with Lord Goderich for a while.'

'You are spoiling me with all this attention,' Goderich said happily. 'What do you say to a hand of cards, Lily?'

Emily did not bother to correct him, but got out the cards and settled in for a boring hour of nonsense while Jane went to her room to freshen her toilette.

Sir William Winston, Baronet, was a cousin of Nick's, and not one to boast of either. He was a ne'er-do-well who, having squandered his own patrimony, moved about from one relative to another, seeking some well-dowered lady foolish enough to marry him. His main attractions were his face and his pleasant line of chatter. Hostesses were always happy to have him on hand as an extra partner at balls, or a stand-in for a dinner party guest who could not come at the last minute. His character was tarnished by his careless way with money, but it was not so blackened that mamas feared to let their daughters stand up with him.

He always flirted with Jane, as indeed he flirted with any single lady possessed of a competence. She was in the mood to have a handsome gentleman make a little fuss over her. Her bruised pride welcomed it. As it was approaching dinnertime, she decided to make her toilette before going downstairs. She had brought a bronze taffeta gown with a gauze overskirt for Christmas dinner. She unbound her hair and brushed it to a burnished copper, then wound it up in a fancier style than she normally wore, and fastened pearl combs on either side. Her mama's topaz necklace matched the gown. It was an old family heirloom, an intricate pendant with topazes set in silver filigree, suspended from a heavy silver chain. It lent a medieval touch to her ensemble.

As she surveyed herself in the mirror, she admitted she was not so lovely as Aurelia, but she thought her more mature, sophisticated appearance might appeal to Sir William. She heard the buzz of conversation from the Gold Saloon as she approached the bottom of the stairs. Sir William was standing just inside the doorway. He turned and looked up at her, then a smile of appreciation lit his handsome, slightly dissipated face.

It was mainly his eyes that one noticed. They were dark, flashing eyes, set in a thin, rather pale, delicately molded face. He was blond, tall, and slender, and wore his clothes with an ease that even Brummell might have envied. Whatever financial scrapes he was in, he never let his toilette suffer. He came forward, leaving the saloon to greet Jane.

'Jane,' he said, bowing. 'The years are kind to you. Like a vintage wine, you improve with aging.' While he spoke, his dark eyes moved admiringly over her Titian hair, down to her topaz necklace and bronze gown.

'Your compliments, on the other hand, deteriorate,' she replied, smiling archly. 'You must know it is not kind to call a lady's attention to her age once she is beyond her teens.'

'I stand corrected. The comparison was wrong on two scores. It is brandy you remind me of, not wine.' He inclined his head to hers and added in a conspiratorial manner, 'They say, you know, that wine is for boys, and brandy for men.'

He offered her his arm to escort her into the saloon. At the archway he stopped and glanced up at the mistletoe, but decided that would be rushing it. But over all he found his interest in Jane quickening.

'You could have knocked me over with a feather when I heard of Nick's engagement,' he said. 'Little Aurelia is doing pretty well for herself.'

'You know her?' Jane asked, surprised. His using her first name suggested a certain degree of intimacy.

'I know the family. I met Aurelia at a party the Huddlestons had a few months ago. I thought at the time she was wasted in such company.' Then he laughed. 'Myself not excluded. I am most often to be found amongst the cits and merchants these days. I have lowered my sights from the aristocracy. A well-dowered cit's daughter will do fine for me. Unless you would like to have me?' he asked, with a glittering smile.

Jane didn't bother answering. She was familiar with his flirtatious ways.

'Are you staying to dinner, Sir William?' she asked.

'Sir William? Oh, come, my dear Jane. I hope we are on closer terms than that. Call me Willie. Everyone does. To answer your question, I plan to stay for dinner. Lady Elizabeth invited me at church this morning. I "misunderstood" her,' he said, with a knowing grin, 'and came with my trunk to spend a few days. Cousin Margaret's place, where I have been staying, is a little crowded. She has her flock home for the holidays.'

He got two glasses of sherry and moved to a sofa a little away from the others for a private cose with Jane.

'Do you know,' he said, gazing at her, 'I always thought you and Nick . . . Am I embarrassing you? Sorry, but surely you must have been shocked to hear of this hasty engagement?'

'Everyone was surprised,' she admitted.

'I should think so. Good God, one trembles to think of the Huddleston *ménage* moving into Clareview *en masse*. Aurelia tells me they are coming for the New Year's ball.'

'It is only a party, not a ball, but yes, Aurelia invited her family. She seems to think her brother cannot be spared when her papa will be away, and one sister, I believe, is increasing and will not be able to travel. Her parents and the Huddlestons should be coming.'

'I would not miss that for a wilderness of monkeys,' he said, and smiled as if at some private joke. Then he cocked an eyebrow at her. 'I see you are too nice to ask. And I am too nice to tell the whole, but let us just say – I don't think they will fit in at Clareview.'

'One never knows. Perhaps they will fit in admirably.'

'Yes, and perhaps there will be roses blooming in the garden tomorrow, but it is not likely. I shall do what I can to pour oil on the waters, of course. *Ça va sans dire.* To tell the truth, I am surprised at Nick's acuity in latching on to the Townsends.'

'I don't believe Nick sees the marriage in that light. He is marrying Aurelia, not the Townsends.'

'You don't walk amongst burdock without picking up burrs.'

'Why do you speak of acuity?'

'The dot must be fabulous.'

From the tail of his eye, Sir William noticed that Nick was keeping a sharp eye on him. If it were Aurelia he were flirting with, he could have understood it, but why was he jealous of his making up to Jane? Was it possible Nick still felt something for her? She was certainly looking extremely handsome this evening. Much more to his own taste than the peaches-and-cream charms of Miss Aurelia.

He decided to test his theory. He took Jane's hand and held it. 'That is a pretty trinket,' he said, using an insignificant pearl ring as an excuse to hold her hand.

'I had it from my grandmama,' she said, gazing fondly at the ring. 'I don't remember her. She must have been small. This was her engagement ring, but it only fits on my little finger.'

'Yet you have small hands,' Sir William said, running his fingers over her hand.

As he watched from the side of his eye, Nicholas detached himself from the grate and came pacing toward him.

# Chapter Eight

$\mathcal{N}$ick wore a smile, but his stiff-legged gait betrayed his annoyance to Sir William, who was an expert at irate gentlemen. Fiancés, fathers, brothers, and husbands – he had dealt with them all in his long career. He was also adept at appeasing their wrath. The first step was an air of innocence, the second an explanation, in this case of the hand-holding episode.

'Jane was just showing me her grandmama's ring,' he said. 'Of course, you would be familiar with it, Nick? Jane has to wear it on her smallest finger, yet it was an engagement ring.'

Nick, feeling rather foolish, looked at the ring. 'I believe I have seen it before,' he said.

'We have not seen Miss Aurelia's ring,' Sir William said, deftly turning the conversation from himself and Jane. He turned and smiled at Aurelia, who rose and joined the group.

'No, I had planned to give her my mama's engagement ring, but she has her heart set on a solitaire, like her sister's,' Nick said. He seated Aurelia and sat beside her. 'We are just discussing your engagement ring,' he explained to his fiancée.

'You are taking chances, letting this lovely little lady walk about without a ring to let the gents know she is taken,' Winston said playfully.

'Our engagement was a spur-of-the-moment thing,' Nick explained. 'There was not time to buy a ring in London.'

'There are some fine estate pieces in the Goderich collection, I recall,' Sir William said. 'Your aunt's diamond, for instance, is a solitaire. What is it, ten carats? A beautiful piece. You should give your fiancée that ring. She will be showered with all the Goderich jewelry. You will have rings on your fingers and bells on your toes, Miss Aurelia.'

Jane noticed he called Aurelia by the more formal name in front of Nick.

'That ring is not mine,' Nick said.

'You are Goderich's heir,' Sir William pointed out. 'Ownership is a mere formality now. He is in no shape to know what is going on, and would not object if he did.'

Nick frowned at this speech. 'I am only his probable heir. His nephew, not his son. My uncle's condition is not so bad as you seem to think, Willie. He improves every day. He might just surprise us and recover, take a young wife, and produce a son of his own.'

'Surely that is not likely!' Willie exclaimed.

'Not likely, but not entirely impossible either,' Nick said. 'I notice a marked improvement in his condition since my return.'

'Well, by Jove,' Willie said, laughing. 'That would be a facer. Mind you, it wouldn't be the first time such a thing happened. You remember Cousin Orville Mersey? He married his young housekeeper when he was seventy-three, had a son and daughter, and diddled young Cousin Harry out of the lot.'

'Our housekeeper is safe,' Nick joked. 'She is already married.'

'Aye, but I see you have unwisely brought in Mrs Lipton,' Willie said, in the same jocular mood. 'Now, there is a temptation for a lonely fellow like Goderich. I must go up and see for myself how he is coming along. Which room is he in?'

'The master bedchamber, of course,' Nick replied.

'I'll go with you, Willie,' Jane offered.

'Going to try your hand with Uncle, are you?' Nick said, still in a bantering tone.

'You had best have Miss Aurelia show me the route instead,' Sir William suggested.

Both Jane and Nick were surprised when Aurelia fell in with this plan, as her aversion to the sickroom was well known by this time.

'Yes, I shall go with you, Willie,' she said. 'I have been wanting to talk to you. Did you call on Marie and Horace before you left?'

They left, chatting like old friends. Nick looked surprised.

'Willie is a friend of the Huddlestons,' Jane explained. 'He has known Aurelia for some months, as a friend of the family, you know.'

'I see,' Nick said. 'Odd I did not run into him at the Huddlestons', but very likely he has been out of town. Perhaps Aurelia will want to invite him to her New Year's party.'

'Yes, I expect she would like that.' She would let Aurelia drop her fiancé the hint that Willie would spend the intervening week at Clareview as well.

As Sir William and Aurelia mounted the grand staircase, she said, 'I shall just take you to the door, Willie. I don't like visiting sick people. Do you think he might really get better and have a son?'

'Probably not. Would it bother you if he did? Nick is not penniless, you know. His own papa left him pretty well to grass.'

'Oh, Willie, you know it is not the money,' she said.

'The title, then?'

'I love Nick, with or without a title. He looked so handsome this morning in his scarlet jacket.' She gave a luxurious little sigh. 'Still, it would be nice to be Lady Goderich. Mama and Papa were so excited when Nick offered for me. None of the others married into the nobility. Marie says it is all the crack to have a big old estate like this in the country. I had looked forward to having big family parties here, after I get the place fixed up, of course. Marie will be a great help in that respect. I quite blush to think of the family seeing all the tatty old carpets and dark pictures. Perhaps something can be done in the intervening week. I hope you will stay and help me, Willie. I know Nick will be busy about the estate. I want him to take care of all the little chores so that we can go to Paris for a nice long honeymoon. You will know what sort of things are in good taste.'

Sir William was overcome by the quantity of ammunition that had just come his way. Every word she uttered gave a prospect of throwing them together, and showed clearly that Nick was making a dreadful mistake in marrying the chit. Aunt Lizzie had told him Nick planned to settle down and take the reins of Clareview, yet Aurelia spoke of jaunting about Paris and London. And when they were here, she would have the house full of vulgar cits. To think of her yanking out the priceless carpets, which belonged in museums, and installing God only knew what, was enough to make him bilious. Whatever his faults, Sir William had good taste, and could not like to think of Clareview being desecrated.

'Everything in the house is in the best of taste, Aurelia,' he said.

'Oh yes. I was not criticizing, it is only that it has all become so old and dark-looking. Just look at these horrid paintings,' she said, pointing at a pair of portraits of a former Lord and Lady Goderich, said to have been painted in the seventeenth century by Van Dyck, that graced the walls of the staircase, nearly disappearing in shadows.

'They are priceless Van Dycks!'

'Really? A pity they are so ugly.'

'Ugly? The models, perhaps, are not beautiful, but the rendering of them is exquisite.' He peered more closely, but unable to see details, he spoke of his knowledge of other Van Dycks. 'Such a delicate use of coloring, and the poses so natural. He had abandoned his Rubenesque tricks by the time he was painting in England. See how Lady Goderich is casually plucking a rose from the bush. You must learn to appreciate fine things, my dear. But actually these particular paintings will not be part of Nick's patrimony. They belong to Lady Elizabeth. Likely she will take them with her to the Dower House when you marry. You really ought to try to hang on to them. She might give them to some other relatives. They belong at Clareview.'

Aurelia listened to every word. She knew her faults and wished to learn about her new home.

When they reached the top of the staircase she said, 'That is old Goderich's room on the right. Let me know how he is coming on. You don't think he might marry and have a son?' she asked again.

'Look at it this way, *ma petite*. If he does, you will not have to live with the tatty old carpets and ugly Van Dycks.'

He strolled along to Lord Goderich's room, where he found the old man standing at the window, enjoying a glass of ale.

'Merry Christmas!' Goderich hollered at him. Goderich didn't recognize him, but he was not entirely incoherent either. Physically he seemed to be in good enough shape. Most troublesome of all, he kept harping on women. A man didn't need a brain to father a child.

'The house is crawling with beautiful women,' he said. 'I don't know where they came from. They come in all colors. Blondes, brunettes, redheads.' This was not incoherent rambling. Aurelia, Mrs Lipton, and Jane were the ladies he meant. 'I mean to have my valet get me into a jacket for this party Ronald is rigging up for New Year's. The redhead tells me I must have a shave and a haircut.'

'There is life in the old boy yet, eh?'

'I fancy the redhead,' Goderich said, with a cagey grin. 'I like a big woman. A good armful. I thought Ronald would have the wits to nab her, but he tells me he is to marry the blonde wench. Ronald is back from the wars, you know. I helped to win it by raising donkeys. He came up to show me his uniform. The blonde chit's papa is a publican. Not the thing, really. I wish you would talk Ronnie out of it.'

Willie stayed long enough to have a glass of ale with the old man before returning belowstairs. Goderich's mind was not perfect, but other than a few confusions, he understood how matters stood. He had raised donkeys for Spain; that was not mere rambling, though he had never actually sent any to Wellington. He knew, at least, that Aurelia Townsend was not a suitable mistress for Clareview.

The dinner bell summoned Sir William back downstairs. The table was trimmed with evergreen boughs and red bows, and laden with the traditional Christmas feast of roast beef, roasted crab, plum pudding, and mince pies. Wine flowed freely, putting everyone in a festive mood, yet there was an undercurrent of uneasiness at the table.

Aurelia was wondering what her family would think of her match if Nick was not to be Lord Goderich, and was not to own Clareview. It still rankled, too, that she could not be married at St. George's in Hanover Square. Pelham noticed that Jane spent more of her time talking to Sir William than himself. Sir William watched them all like a spy, wondering how he might maneuver the unstable situation here to his advantage. He was not imagining that Nick was jealous of his *à suivie* flirtation with Jane. Nick's dark eyes turned in their direction more often than chance would dictate. Nicholas was the most confused of all. Aurelia had suggested, before dinner, that they should make a long stay in Paris for their honeymoon. He kept telling himself that he was madly in love with her. His eyes told him that she was ravishingly beautiful; his body told him that he wanted her. Surely his great love affair was more than mere animal lust?

Certainly he had felt the bristling heat of jealousy when she went so happily upstairs with Willie. Yet he had experienced the same sensation when Willie was holding Jane's hand. It was bad enough that Pelham was showing signs of infatuation for Jane. He was a fool, but a good-natured, well-to-do one at least. Willie was a scoundrel – the sort of scoundrel whom the ladies seemed to find irresistible. At least he would be leaving after dinner. He couldn't do much mischief in a couple of hours.

While these thoughts whirled through his brain, the table talk continued apace. He shook himself to attention and listened to what Aurelia was saying.

'Is that not wonderful news, Nick? Willie has agreed to stay for our New Year's party. Marie will be surprised to find him here. She thinks he is *her cicisbeo*.'

Before he could reply, Lady Elizabeth said, 'Do stay, Willie.' Even she was not immune to the scoundrel's flashing eyes. 'In fact, you must stay on for the wedding. You will be no end of help in all the little chores that pile up in arranging parties. I remember what an invaluable assistance you were for our May ball the second year Nick was gone. The orchestra, the wine, the decorations – we could not have done it without you.'

'You are too kind, Aunt Lizzie. I shall be happy to stay, if I can be of assistance.'

'Then it is settled,' Lizzie said, smiling graciously.

Lady Elizabeth was the mistress of the house. Nick could hardly object. He smiled and said halfheartedly, 'That is good of you, Willie.'

Willie breathed a sigh of relief. There was no need to claim he felt ill, which would involve at least one day in bed. No need, either, to tell them his trunk was already unpacked. 'I shall send my valet to Margaret's place for the rest of my things. He came to help me dress for dinner.'

After dinner the ladies retired to the Gold Saloon. Lizzie said to Aurelia, 'You must start thinking what you would like for a wedding gift, my dear. I want to give you and Nick something to remember me by.'

After a pause for consideration, Aurelia said, 'Perhaps Nick would like the Van Dyck portraits on the staircase to stay at Clareview. I understand they belong to you. Since they are portraits of ancestors, you know, it would be nice to keep them here. But if you would prefer to take them with you to the

Dower House, that is all right,' she added dutifully.

Lady Elizabeth felt a pang at that heartless mention of her removing to the Dower House. Clareview did not belong to Nick yet. She was Goderich's sister and had every right to remain. The Van Dycks were a different matter entirely. She felt she ought to tell Aurelia they were only copies. It was not generally known that the originals had been lost a hundred years ago when a fire consumed the east wing of the house, and copies made at the time by a local artist.

'Oh, I don't think you would want them,' she felt obliged to demur. 'They are—'

'Oh, indeed I do appreciate fine things,' Aurelia assured her. 'They are so lovely. Typical of Van Dyck's English period, don't you think? After he had got rid of Rubens's influence. Very natural-looking, with that fine brushwork.'

Mrs Lipton and Lady Elizabeth exchanged a frowning look. It seemed impossible to tell the chit that the paintings were only copies. It would make her look a fool.

'I shall be happy to give them to you,' Lizzie said. She would ask Nick about what present he would like. Naturally she would leave the copies of the Van Dycks at Clareview. She was not a savage, to be removing historical items from their home. Besides, she thought they were ugly.

'When do you think your family will be arriving for the New Year's party, Aurelia?' Mrs Lipton asked.

'I wrote to them yesterday. I expect Marie will send a special messenger with her answer. I may hear tomorrow.'

'I must have the guest rooms turned out,' Lizzie said.

The conversation turned to domestic matters and passed peacefully until the gentlemen joined them.

# Chapter Nine

$\mathcal{T}$he remainder of the evening passed pleasantly. It was not until the next morning that the first cracks appeared on the smooth surface of relations at Clareview. Aurelia was unhappy to hear that Nicholas meant to spend the morning with his agent, Fogarty, riding over the estate to see various changes and improvements made during his absence. He didn't tell her that he must spend the afternoon going over the accounts and discussing the running of Clareview.

'You and Jane can begin planning the New Year's party,' he said, to placate the sulking Aurelia, before leaving. 'Aunt Lizzie will have a list somewhere about the house. Jane will know if there are some younger people who should be added to it.'

Aurelia replied, 'I had planned to go to the village this morning to buy a few things for the party, you know. To smarten us up.'

'An excellent idea,' Lizzie said. 'Emily and I will write the invitations, Nick. Youngsters like to be out and doing.'

'Very happy to help,' Mrs Lipton agreed.

'In that case, I am sure Jane would like to accompany you to

Amberley,' Nick said to Aurelia. In his innocence, he thought his fiancée wanted to buy ribbons or scent or some ladies' trifles.

'Perhaps she should come with us,' she said. 'Willie offered to go with me. It might look odd if the villagers saw me on the strut with a young man without a chaperon.'

It was pretty clear to Nick that Aurelia saw Willie as an eligible gentleman, despite the fifteen-year difference in their ages. Only Willie noticed the stiffening of Jane's spine to be charged with playing chaperon.

'You will keep me in line, Jane,' he said, laughing. 'But who will chaperon the chaperon?'

'You are quite safe from me, Willie,' Jane replied.

'Pity,' he murmured, with a flashing glance. Nick was not amused at this bantering. 'You might ask Pel to go with you, Jane,' he said. Safety in numbers.

As soon as breakfast was over, Aurelia herded the group into Nick's carriage and they drove off to Amberley. This quaint spot was considered a pattern card of village beauty. The cottages, with their facades of timber, brick, clunch, and flint, were typical of the area. Smoke streamed from the chimneys of the tidy thatched and tile roofs, lending a homey touch.

'That is my church, where you will be married,' Pelham said, pointing out the same church they had attended the day before.

'It is very small,' Aurelia said, frowning.

'It's a small village,' Pel said.

'Indeed it is.' She looked forlornly at the small houses and few little shops. 'I doubt I will be able to find decent carpets here.'

'Carpets?' Sir William asked, staring. He looked at Jane, who was also showing alarm.

'I am ashamed to have my family see those horrid threadbare

things at Clareview. I must smarten the place up before they come. I daresay there is not time to have new draperies made.'

'That would take a few weeks,' Jane said firmly.

'Jed Williams sells all kinds of furnishings, along with carpets,' Pelham said.

Jane gave him a meaningful look. 'It might be best to consult with Lady Elizabeth and Nick before buying carpets,' she said.

'Oh, I don't want Nick to know. It is a surprise,' Aurelia said, 'but I told him I wanted to smarten the place up, and he thinks it is a good idea. It won't cost him a penny. Papa is giving me money for a wedding gift. I can put it on his account, and he will pay for it when he comes.'

Jane tugged at Sir William's sleeve, as he seemed to have some influence over the girl.

'No harm to look,' he said, with a wink over Aurelia's shoulder to reassure Jane he would not let her buy anything.

Jed Williams's goods were purveyed to villagers and the more prosperous farmers with a taste for finery. They were gaudy, cheap imitations of Persian carpets, with a price to match.

'I am surprised Aunt Lizzie has let the place go to rack and ruin when these nice carpets are going for an old ballad,' Aurelia said, gazing in satisfaction at the floor coverings. 'A pity they are so small. It will take two or three to cover the Gold Saloon. What do you think, Willie? Handsome, are they not?'

'Very handsome,' he said, in a choked voice, 'but let us look around before making up our minds.'

'There's no other place that sells carpets,' Pelham told them. 'I bought one of these myself to brighten up a spare bedroom. It holds up well. Mind you, no one has used the room yet.'

'I think if we buy two, they will do nicely,' Aurelia said.

'Do you know, I have just been thinking,' Sir William said, with a well-simulated air of spontaneity, 'we are only a stone's throw from Brighton. Why do we not jog over to Brighton tomorrow, Aurelia? They are bound to have a better quality of goods there, and more variety.'

'Could we not go this afternoon?' she asked. 'There is no saying. My family may be arriving tomorrow'

'I doubt they will come quite that soon,' he said. 'If I know Marie, she will want to have a new gown made up for the party.'

'That is true,' she said, nodding. 'I shall have Nick take me to Brighton tomorrow. You must come with us, for I fear Nick hasn't much taste in household decorating. I am so glad you are here to advise me, Willie. I don't know what I should do without you.' She walked along with Willie. Drawing ahead of the others, she continued in a confidential tone, 'Those two, you must know, are quite hopeless. Jane has worn the same afternoon gown ever since I have been at Clareview. I expect she is poor, but I like her. I do not lord it over her, I promise you.'

'She is not so well to grass as yourself,' Willie allowed. Really the chit was impossible. His instinct was to give her her head, let her buy up every tawdry item in town and dump them at Clareview. That ought to be enough to show Nick what he was in for. His innate taste prevented him from following this course.

He tried another tack instead. 'The one you really ought to consult is Aunt Lizzie. She is the mistress of Clareview. You and Nick will be staying there as her guests, of course, but—'

Aurelia gave an exasperated sigh. 'When Nick said he wanted me to see his home, I assumed it belonged to him. I cannot like to think of living in another lady's house. Eleanor – you have not met my second oldest sister yet – Eleanor had to live with her mama-in-law for a year, until she started her nursery. She said it was the worst year of her life. She cried so hard, Papa had to build her and Samuel their own place.'

'Then you can always try tears, if you find you cannot stay the course at Clareview.'

'The whole point of marrying Nick was to be a countess, and have a country estate. Now it seems – Not that I do not love him!' she added. 'Indeed I am very fond of Nick. Did you see him in his regimentals at church yesterday?'

'Yes, he looked magnificent.'

'Everyone was staring at us.'

'I fancy everyone stares at you, wherever you go,' Willie replied. 'Just look at how the villagers are staring now.'

She looked around and saw that it was true. She didn't require Nick to claim attention. Everyone was gazing at her in admiration. It put her back into spirits.

Jane suggested they go into Codey's Drapery Shop, hoping to limit Aurelia's shopping to personal items. Aurelia was easily diverted by this ploy. As long as she could be buying something, she was happy.

'Look at the lovely blue silk stockings,' she said, snapping them up. 'They will just match the blue suit I am having made for my trousseau. And silver buttons! I did not think to find such treasures in a little place like this. Dear me, I cannot remember whether the suit takes six buttons or twelve.'

'Surely not so many as twelve,' Jane said.

'It has a double row of buttons. You must have seen the suit in *La Belle Assemblée* – the one with the small waist and flounced jacket. I had best take a dozen, to be sure.'

She found other treasures, enough to endear her to the hearts of the Codeys, and provide gossip in Amberley for a fortnight, for it is not to be expected the local ladies were content with one glance at her on the street. Several of them followed her into the store to spy on her.

When she had relieved Codey's of its more elegant trifles, she suggested they take lunch at the inn.

'We did not tell Lady Elizabeth we'd be away for lunch,' Jane reminded her.

'I shall take her home a box of bonbons. That will turn her up sweet, if she is a little out of curl.'

'The bonbons are an excellent idea,' Willie replied, 'but it would be unladylike to remain away for lunch without inform-ing your hostess.'

Eating at the inn was not mentioned again. Aurelia was a quick enough learner, but she did insist on stopping for a cup of tea at least, since there were so few shops to entertain her.

'There is an antique store at the far end of town,' Jane mentioned. 'They have some rather nice things.'

Aurelia gave her a cool look. 'I don't buy secondhand merchandise, Jane. It will be more convenient shopping in Brighton, actually. We spent a month there last summer, and the merchants know me.'

Willie directed a wink at Jane.

'That's that, then. Let us have a nice cup of tea,' Pelham said, and headed across the street to the inn.

When they returned to Clareview, lunch passed without incident. Aurelia gave Lady Elizabeth her bonbons, saying, 'We wanted to take lunch in town, but as we forgot to mention it to you, of course, we could not. I should mention that tomorrow we will be away for luncheon. I must go to Brighton to do some shopping.'

'More shopping.' Nick looked a question at her.

'Can you come with me, Nick?' she asked.

'I am pretty busy. Perhaps—'

'I don't want to interrupt your work. You attend to all the farming details so that you are free for our honeymoon. Willie has offered to take me, if you are too busy.'

Nick was torn in two directions. He disliked shopping quite as much as most gentlemen, yet he felt he should accompany her, and felt even more strongly that Willie was seeing too much of his fiancée. He assumed that Jane and Pel would be along. He would ask Jane to keep an eye on Aurelia.

'Why Brighton?' Lizzie asked. 'You will find it cold and damp in December, my dear.'

'I have so many items to buy, with my wedding coming on, you know, and the shops there are wonderful.'

After lunch, Nick spent the afternoon in the study going over the books with Fogarty, while the others began arranging the New Year's party.

'Perhaps you would be kind enough to deliver the invitations, Willie,' Nick suggested, to keep him away from Aurelia. He knew that Willie liked visiting.

Willie accepted this chore with alacrity. He spent a sociable afternoon going from house to house, drinking a glass of wine at each one, flirting with all the eligible ladies, and answering questions about Miss Aurelia.

The ladies and Pelham discussed arrangements for the party.

'I would like the entrance hall and ballroom full of flowers,' Aurelia said.

'There aren't that many flowers in bloom in December,' Jane pointed out. 'We can go to the conservatory and see what the gardener can do for us. I'm sure he can arrange a few vases.'

'Why don't we order them from a florist?' Aurelia asked.

'There is no florist in Amberley,' Jane replied.

'Oh. It is very difficult arranging a party in a place like this, is it not?' Aurelia asked with a *tsk* of impatience.

'It will look very nice. You'll see. We shall leave up the evergreens. James – that's the gardener – will bring in palms from the conservatory, and find enough flowers that we are not disgraced.'

'Is there anyone who can play music for us in Amberley?'

'Oh, yes, that will be no problem. Pel, perhaps you could arrange that with the Wolfe brothers? They have a group who play at all the parties,' Jane explained to Aurelia.

Food and drink, at least, were no problem. Lizzie took charge of that. 'The usual, Mrs Hancock,' she said, and it was understood that lobster patties would be served, along with stuffed fowl, ham, raised pigeon pies, and other dainties.

After dinner, Pelham suggested a game of whist. Aurelia said, 'I don't play cards.'

Upon hearing this, Nick also declined. As he knew his Aunt Lizzie dearly loved a game, however, he urged the scheme on. Jane agreed to partner Pel against Lizzie and Sir William. Mrs Lipton, who did not wish to interrupt her knitting, said she would go abovestairs and keep Goderich company.

'You two won't mind being alone,' she said archly to Nick and Aurelia.

'Alone – at last,' Nick said, settling in with his fiancée by the grate.

Yet the interval was not as enjoyable as he had hoped. His beloved did a deal of complaining about the lack of shops in Amberley. When this subject was exhausted, she took up a ladies'

magazine to hear his opinion on various gowns and bonnets she
planned to purchase.

'For I don't want to look a dowd on our honeymoon,' she
said. 'I wager the ladies in Paris think of nothing but fashion.'

'I am afraid it will be difficult to get away—'

'Nick! You *promised* you would take me to Paris.'

'I meant in the spring. Winter in Paris would be—'

'It would not be any colder than London. Oh, we must go to
Paris, Nick. I have told all my friends and family we are going. It
will be marvelous. Wellington there as ambassador, and you close
as inkle-weavers with him. He will introduce us to everyone. It
is too good a chance to miss.'

'But there is so much to do about the estate. I have been away
for three years, and with Goderich ill—' Nick had had enough of
travel. He had been looking forward to coming home and
settling down.

She pokered up. 'I have agreed to be married in the country,
when you know perfectly well I wanted to have the wedding at
St. George's. You must let me have something my own way.'

'We'll have the wedding in London,' he said, opting for the
quicker way of getting home.

'Oh, thank you, Nick!' she said, and placed a kiss on his cheek.
'And we shall leave for Paris the next day.'

'I meant have the wedding in London instead of going to Paris.'

Her lower lip began to wobble. 'Oh, I see. Why can't we do
both? Have the wedding in London and go to Paris? I have never
been to Paris. I have never been anywhere. I would rather go to
Paris than be married at St. George's.'

Nick felt a perfect brute. He was being selfish. Just because he
was tired of travel was no reason to rob Aurelia of a visit abroad.

But he really could not leave immediately. Goderich, in his senility, had taken some freakish notions about managing the estate. When Nick had written him about using donkeys in Spain as they stood up to the hot climate better than horses, Goderich had insisted on raising donkeys, to the detriment of the cattle. He had three dozen donkeys in the barn, eating their heads off and offering very little possibility of profit.

Fogarty had told him of some excellent milchers going up for auction in January. Nick wanted to attend that auction, and pick out the prime ones for breeding. There were dozens of other matters that needed immediate attention as well. Fields to be drained and marled, the barns to be repaired.

'I'll take you to Paris in the spring,' he said. Whether this would give him his wedding in Amberley was not mentioned. 'That is a promise, Aurelia. I cannot leave now. There is too much to do. We don't want to run the estate into the ground. It is our future.'

'Yes, if old Goderich doesn't marry and have a son. You don't have to worry about money, Nick. Papa—'

'Don't be ridiculous! Marry, at his age, and in his condition? I don't intend to become your papa's pensioner,' he said sharply.

'Don't worry, it wouldn't be a gift. He'd make you work for your money. Eleanor's husband has taken over the Manchester brewery, but Papa plans to open another one in Kent. You would be perfect to run it.'

Nick just stared. 'I don't know anything about brewing ale, nor do I have the least interest in learning.'

'It is a deal more certain than farming,' she snipped. 'Papa says farming is the worst investment a man can make. It takes so much land, and you are at the mercy of the weather and diseases and blights and corn prices . . . Whatever the weather, everyone likes his ale.'

Nick sat silent a moment, thinking. All these matters must be thrashed out between them, but in private, not with Jane and Lizzie and Willie casting those questioning looks from the card table.

He picked up the magazine and said, 'Show me that bonnet again, the one with the pink feathers. You would look adorable in it.'

That easily was Aurelia diverted from discussing her future, and Nick's. 'I shall have the milliner put on blue feathers, of course. Pink is vulgar, don't you think?'

'Blue suits you better. It matches your eyes.' Oh, Lord! Was he doomed to a lifetime of these platitudes? His eyes strayed to the card table, where a lively argument had broken out.

'If you want my opinion, which you don't, I think you reneged,' Pelham was saying to Willie.

'So succinctly put, Pelham,' Willie replied. 'I can only wonder why, when you discerned my lack of interest in your opinion, you insisted on giving it.'

'Because you reneged.'

Nick wished he were at the table. He liked a good, argumentative game of cards. Jane, as he might have expected, soon brought order to the chaos.

'Let us deal a fresh hand. And next time, Master Jackanapes,' she added in a playful aside to Willie, 'we shall all be keeping a sharp eye on you. You are forewarned.'

Willie inclined his head to Jane's and said, smiling, 'Then I shall keep the other two aces up my sleeve.'

Jane made some light response. How pretty she looked. Her little flirtation with Willie brought a sparkle to her eyes. She was not immune to Willie's charm, despite her knowledge of his circumstances. He would steal her from Pelham, if Pel wasn't careful.

How complicated this game of love was. A moment's infatuation leading to a declaration, and one's fate was sealed. He had come home from Spain, eager to get to Clareview, only to be pressured by Wellington into doing liaison work in London while Wellington went to Paris. He had met Aurelia and been bowled over by her beauty. She was young and friendly, and seemed exactly the bride he wanted to take home to Clareview. She had probably been attracted by the romance of his having been a colonel, back from the war, a protégé of Wellington. She wanted what he was tired of.

And now they were more or less stuck with each other. He would never be that carefree young soldier again. And she would never really be happy here, away from the only life she had ever known. She had been born and raised in a city. She didn't ride, she didn't even like dogs. Cutting a swath in society was her aim. And the fault was his. She was young and inexperienced. He was older and ought to have been wiser. They must reach some compromise. Perhaps when she started the nursery she would take more interest in Clareview.

# Chapter Ten

$\mathcal{M}$rs Lipton had a touch of flu the next morning. Although she came down to breakfast, her flushed face was enough to cause her hostess concern.

'Emily, you have gone and caught Goderich's cold,' Lizzie said.

'I expect I did catch it from Lord Goderich,' she said. 'He was coughing last night.'

'You want to be well for the party, Emily. You must go straight to bed.'

'I promised James I would help him with the flowers in the conservatory. It is nice and warm there. Perhaps I could—'

'No, no. Bed is the place for you,' Lizzie insisted.

'I don't feel much like eating. I believe I will go and lie down for a few hours, if you would tell James, Jane.'

'I shall take your place in the conservatory,' Jane offered.

As soon as this was settled, Aurelia said, 'Will you be coming to Brighton with me, Nick?'

'I'm afraid I cannot get away. I wish you will not go, my dear. With this flu going around – and Brighton is cold.'

'I simply must go shopping,' she insisted, looking to Willie for support.

Willie shrugged his shoulders. 'You two battle it out between you. Never let it be said I stuck in my oar between lovers. If you decide to go, I shall be happy to accompany you.'

'There you are, then. Willie will go with you,' Lady Elizabeth said, and it was settled.

'Pel, will you go with them?' Nick asked.

Pel felt his throat and coughed. 'I believe I have a touch of whatever is going around myself.'

'Good gracious!' Lizzie exclaimed. 'We are all falling like flies, and with a party to prepare. Perhaps we should cancel it.'

Aurelia looked up, horrified. 'I have had a reply to my invitations this morning, Aunt Lizzie. Mama and Papa are coming the day of the ball. Papa has postponed an important business meeting to come, and the Huddlestons will be arriving tomorrow. We cannot cancel the party.'

'That would be nearly as much bother as going forth with it,' Willie said. 'The invitations have been delivered, the musicians hired, Cook has begun preparing the food. Surely there is no need to cancel. I had a touch of this cold myself last week. It passes in no time. I guarantee the invalids will be well in a day or two. What do you think, Nick?'

Aurelia's wobbling lip told Nick what he was to think. 'Let us go ahead with it. It is half-arranged,' he said.

She smiled at him. 'I shall wear my new ball gown.'

'Oh, it is not a ball, my dear,' Lizzie reminded her. 'Nothing too grand. The gown you wore on Christmas Eve would do admirably.'

'That old thing?' Aurelia asked. 'Everyone has seen it.'

Lady Elizabeth blinked in astonishment. Everyone had been seeing her magenta crepe for a decade, which did not mean they would not be seeing it again on New Year's Eve, and for another decade.

Nick read the shock on all the faces staring at his beloved, and was angry with them all. He was angry with Aurelia, and with himself. Why couldn't they understand? Why couldn't she?

'Don't leave your departure for Brighton too late, Aurelia,' he said, rather curtly. 'It is coming on dark by four o'clock. You will want to leave Brighton by three, at the latest. What is so urgent that you must go today?'

'It's a surprise, Nick,' she said. He thought she meant to buy him some bauble.

'I don't much care for surprises,' he said, hoping still to prevent the visit.

'You will like this one,' she said.

Willie saw that he would have to provide a luncheon, preferably in the smartest inn at Brighton. This posed a problem, as his pockets were to let. He had a word with Lady Elizabeth before leaving.

'I had not planned to be away from Clareview,' he said, blushing. 'I didn't visit the bank before leaving London. I wonder if you could lend me a couple of pounds.'

This was no new thing with Willie Winston. He usually forgot to visit his bank, and forgot to repay his loans as well, but Aurelia had her heart set on the little trip, and since Nick would be busy, Lizzie was just as happy to have the girl out of the house. She seemed a restless little creature. Even, Lizzie was coming to think, removing to the Dower House was not a bad idea. She gave Willie five pounds. He kissed her cheek and told her she was a darling.

He and Aurelia left early, promising to be home before dark. They spent a thoroughly enjoyable day, visiting the shops and buying a great many expensive items. The merchants made no demur when told to send the bill to Mr Edward Townsend, and forward the merchandise to Clareview. Willie enjoyed having merchants fawn over him. It was an entirely new sensation. He steered her away from the gaudier items that attracted her. The pair of lamps with dangling crystals, he assured her, were so fine, they would make the rest of the Gold Saloon look shabby. The pair of French lamps with the Meissen painted bases were in better taste.

He had learned that the magic words "vulgar" and "in poor taste" worked like a charm with her. That she was refurbishing a house that did not belong to her to impress her relatives would be enough vulgarity and poor taste to cause dismay at Clareview. He was not responsible for Aurelia's behavior, but the actual selections in some part reflected on him, and he valued his aesthetic reputation.

Willie could be charming when he set his mind to it. It did not bother him one whit that Aurelia was headstrong, vain, and vulgar. She was young and trainable. Over lunch, she confessed that Nick was being impossible. Willie encouraged her in her sentiment of being badly used.

'In a marriage, you should begin as you mean to go on,' he said in an avuncular way, filling her wineglass.

'That is exactly what Marie told me. I felt a little uncertain when I first arrived at Clareview, with so many strangers about, but now that they all like me, it is time to show my mettle. I daresay it was my agreeing to be married from Clareview that made Nick think I have no backbone. If he thinks to weasel out of the honeymoon in Paris, he is badly mistaken. Who is to say Wellington will still be there in the spring? I quite count on Wellington to be our sponsor into society.'

Willie did not think a distinguished colonel and Lord Goderich's heir required a sponsor, but he did not say so. 'Quite right, my dear. Nick does not really know how to treat a lady. He was too long in Spain. It was bound to cause a few rough edges. These gentlemen farmers, you know, care for nothing but cows and pigs.'

'Horrid smelly things. Why can they not just buy their mutton in a civilized way?'

'Have a little more of this chicken.' He placed it tenderly on her plate. 'As to the cows and pigs, you had best learn to love them. You will have uphill work getting Nick away from Clareview. Oh, I daresay he will take you to London for a week in the Season if you harp at him. Once you start your nursery, of course, it will be harder to get away.'

'A week! Why, he has a mansion on Grosvenor Square. Why should we not stay for the whole Season?'

'That is the busiest season on a farm.'

'I am beginning to hate Clareview,' she said. 'And there is no hope of getting Nick away from it. When I suggested Papa would let him take over the new brewery in Kent, he ground his teeth. Really! He did not say much, but he ground his teeth. The brewery is to be at Chatham, close to London. Chatham is much livelier than Amberley. What a horrid place that is. Those miserable little shops. And one assembly a month, if you please! Who would there be to go if they had one every night? There is no decent society there.'

She emptied her glass, and Willie filled it. 'It is so good to have someone to talk to,' she said. 'I had thought Jane might prove a friend, but really, you know, she is such a provincial. You must visit me long and often after I am married.'

This was a poor second best to marrying her, but it was not to be despised either. Willie was on close terms with many noble ladies. He was not entirely without principles. He truly thought Aurelia and Nick were a poor match. He, on the other hand, had not the least objection to marrying a pretty widgeon, nor to living in London – or Chatham, for that matter. He rubbed along well with the Huddlestons. A touch of vulgarity did not bother him, so long as it was monied vulgarity. He lent a touch of class to the nouveau riche. They liked being on terms with Sir William Winston, cousin of Lord Goderich and half a dozen other fine lords and ladies. Many a merchant's wife sought his expertise in matters of furnishing her mansion or her country estate. It had become a profitable little business. The purveyors of furnishings, paintings, and carpets were happy to give him a bonus for directing his wealthy friends to them.

Willie studied her for a long, silent moment, his gaze lingering on her fine eyes, her delicate cheeks, her full lips, and sighed. 'I only wish . . .'

'What?' she asked, with a questioning look.

'No, I cannot say it.'

Her expression heightened to eager anticipation. 'You can tell me anything, Willie.'

'You are betrothed. It would be improper.'

She reached across the table and took his hands. 'Dear Willie,' she said, with a smile that would have done credit to the tragic muse Mrs Siddons. 'I think I have an inkling of your meaning. Alas, it was not meant to be, but I will always remember this day. It has been special to me. Very unique.'

'And me, my dear Aurelia,' he said, wincing at that 'very unique.'

She wiped a tear from her eyes.

'What a brute I am!' he said at once. 'We must cheer you up. I have it! A new bonnet. We shall buy you a new bonnet, so that we have something to take back to Clareview, for the carpet and other things will not arrive until tomorrow.'

'Oh, you are thoughtful, Willie. I wager Nick would not have thought of that.'

'But first, some dessert. Sweets for the sweet.' God, had he really said that? 'What do you say to the syllabub?'

She agreed, and had a plate of macaroons with it. After they left the inn, Mr Townsend had a charming bonnet put on his account. Willie counted up his change and decided he could afford a small sentimental token gift. He bought Aurelia a silk fan with a likeness of the prince's pavilion painted on it, and bestowed it on her with all the passion at his command.

'I shall always cherish it as a momentum of this day,' she said.

Willie didn't wince or correct her error.

'Let us go and have a look at the pavilion before leaving,' he suggested.

Fate was on his side. It never entered his head that the Prince Regent would be in Brighton in the middle of the winter. Even if he was, it was unlikely that he would brave the inclement weather, when he was such a devotee of a blazing fire. But Lady Hertford had come to Brighton to visit a sick friend, and it was not to be supposed that this formidable dame would let Prinny off the leash entirely. His carriage was coming down the drive as Willie and Aurelia stood gazing at the collection of domes, minarets, and finials that had added such a burden of taxes to the ratepayers of England. Willie thought its Oriental style looked particularly ludicrous when surrounded with snow.

'Isn't it lovely?' Aurelia sighed.

'Charming.'

The prince recognized Sir William, and seeing the Incomparable with him, gave the drawstring a pull. The carriage stopped. The prince lowered the window and said, 'I say, is that you, Sir William? What the deuce are you doing in Brighton at this time of year?'

'Just showing Miss Townsend your magnificent pavilion, Your Highness,' Sir William said with a bow. His hope that the name Townsend would be recognized, and some little compliment offered, was fulfilled.

'Miss Townsend, eh? Not one of Edward Townsend's daughters?' Miss Townsend was shaking like a blancmange, but she managed to curtsy low. 'She is dashed pretty. My compliments of the season, Miss Townsend. I enjoy your papa's brew.'

He nodded graciously, raised the window, and continued on his way, while Miss Aurelia stood gazing after the carriage with her mouth open.

'That was the Prince Regent!' she said in a hushed voice.

'Yes.'

'He knew your name!'

'I have played cards with him a few times.'

'Marie will never believe it. I wish I had been wearing my new bonnet.'

She looked at her escort with a respect bordering on awe as

they went to the carriage. She could not think of anything else all the way home but having met the prince.

The shadows were lengthening by four o'clock, when Nick left his office. He met Jane just descending the great staircase.

'Are they back yet?' he asked her.

She peered into the Gold Saloon. 'It seems not. Aurelia is not abovestairs.'

They walked into the saloon. 'How is your aunt?' he asked.

'She is resting. I believe Willie is right, and it is just a mild cold. She has no stomach upset. Your uncle is resting quietly as well.'

Nick couldn't settle down. He poured two glasses of wine, but kept pacing to and fro in front of the fireplace.

'I cannot imagine what is keeping them,' he said. 'I told her to be home before dark.'

'It is not quite dark yet,' she pointed out. 'It always looks darker from a bright room. When you are actually outdoors, it seems brighter somehow.'

'What a debater you would have made.'

'Do sit down, Nick. You are making me nervous with your pacing. She is not alone.'

'That is what concerns me. Willie—'

'Willie is a gentleman,' she said firmly. 'He would never misbehave with a young lady, and certainly not with your fiancée.'

'She should not have gone at this time, with the party to prepare and Uncle sick.'

'You are working yourself into a pelter over nothing. It is not Aurelia's place to prepare the party. The fact is, you are feeling guilty for not having gone with her, and want to place the blame on her.'

Nick gave a sheepish grin. 'I expect you are right. You must keep me in line, Jane. I would appreciate it if you could also pass along some of your common sense to my fiancée. Aurelia is inexperienced. You could guide her – this party, for instance. She has been pestering Lizzie to send to London for flowers and arrange an ice sculpture for the dinner table.'

'Actually, Aurelia has asked my advice. I have told her how country parties are run. I believe she wishes to smarten us up. Perhaps we are in need of it,' she added pensively. 'The neighborhood has always looked to Clareview to set the pace. It will be her role to lead society. How should I presume to teach her, when I have no experience beyond Amberley?'

Nick listened, and had to admit that there was some truth in Jane's reply. Yet he was still not happy. He didn't want to be smartened up. He wanted things to continue as they had always been. He thought of the coming wedding – was it to be at St. George's or at home? And what of the demmed honeymoon?

'I wish—' He bit back the foolish thing he had nearly blurted out. I wish I had never asked Aurelia to marry me.

Jane looked at him curiously. At that moment the front door flew open and Aurelia came rushing in.

'You'll never guess what, Nick!'

'You're late,' he said sternly.

'I met the prince! Willie introduced me to him.' She turned an admiring look on Sir William, who tried to look modest. 'And I bought a new bonnet.'

So that was her great surprise. She had gone pelting off to Brighton without him to buy yet another new bonnet, in the dead of winter, and with a flu going around.

Jane saw the frown darkening his brow; she gave him an

admonishing look and rushed forward. 'You met the prince! How lovely! You must come in and tell us all about it.'

# Chapter Eleven

Until dinnertime, there was but one subject: Aurelia's meeting the prince. Every detail was described at length: how he looked, what sort of carriage he was driven in, what he wore, but most of all, what he said.

'He asked if I was Edward Townsend's daughter, and said I was dashed pretty,' she told Nick, even before removing her bonnet.

By the time she was in the Gold Saloon relating the story for Jane's edification, she had become 'so pretty.'

When the group met for a glass of sherry before dinner, she was overheard telling Pelham the prince had told her she was 'very pretty.'

'Pretty?' Pel asked. 'The man must be blind. Anyone can see you are beautiful.'

'Perhaps that was the word he used,' she said, blushing daintily. 'Do you remember, Willie?'

'I am sure he said beautiful. Dashed beautiful, wasn't it?'

'I wish I could remember.'

It took only the twinkling of a bedpost until she remembered the word the prince had actually used was Incomparable, at which point Willie remembered it, too.

'I own I am surprised,' Lizzie said, 'for in the usual way, what Prinny finds beautiful is older, stout matrons like Lady Hertford. But let us not spoil dinner by speaking of Prinny. We can find a more appetizing topic.'

As country hours were kept at Clareview, dinner was over by seven-thirty, with a long evening to be got in.

When Lizzie said she was going abovestairs to keep Emily company, Pel said, 'There goes our card game, then. What shall we do instead? James has brought in some boughs to decorate the ballroom. Shall we put them up?'

'The servants can do that,' Aurelia said, fanning herself with a silk fan bearing a likeness of the prince's pavilion at Brighton. She picked up one of her many fashion magazines and went to the sofa by the grate.

'The family always hangs the festive boughs,' Nick told her. 'It is a tradition.'

'Our tradition at home is for the servants to do the work,' she replied. 'That is why we hire them.'

'I shall help you, Pel. You come along, too, Willie. We need someone to hold the ladder and someone to climb it,' Jane said, thinking to leave the engaged couple alone to smooth away their troubles. She had noticed at dinner that Nick was still in a brooding mood. Having Willie on his hands wouldn't help.

'I promised Lizzie I would do a stint with the old boy,' Willie replied, meaning Lord Goderich.

'Then Pel and I will do the decorations. We don't really need three people,' Jane said.

Willie picked up the latest journal and left.

'We shall all go,' Nick said, rising to join them. He glanced at Aurelia, who turned a page of her magazine, oblivious to the conversation going forth around her.

'No, no,' Jane replied. 'You keep Aurelia company. Pel and I can handle it.'

'We ain't really family,' Pel said. 'I mean to say, the tradition. Although we hung the boughs while Nick was away.'

'I consider you both honorary family members,' Nick said.

It was clear to Jane, who knew Nick so well, that he was embarrassed at his chosen one's lack of interest in family traditions, or indeed in anything except her magazines. Jane took Pel's hand and led him off.

'I ain't much good at heights,' he muttered, but Jane soon teased him into a good mood.

Nick watched them go, wishing he were with them. He remembered they used to sing carols while hanging the boughs. He recalled the year a mouse had scampered up Pel's leg, and Pel had come crashing down from the ladder when Jane screamed fit to wake the dead. He had thought that effectual lady would whack the mouse with a broom, as he had seen the servants do when he was a young lad. That was the year she had put on long skirts and become a lady. He and Pel had teased her, pretending to see a mouse in every corner to hear her scream. It seemed a hundred years ago.

In the ballroom, Jane saw the servants had brought up a ladder. There were hooks placed high on the wall to hold the boughs.

'Do you want me to go up the ladder?' Jane asked. 'I'm not afraid of heights.'

'I'll do it. It'll be a challenge for me. I like to challenge myself from time to time.'

'Have you challenged your memory yet? To learn the wedding ceremony, I mean?'

'It ain't settled for sure where the wedding will take place. No point learning it for nothing.'

He arranged the ladder beneath the first hook. Jane brought a bough and held the ladder until he had mounted high enough to reach the hook. Then she handed him up the bough. As the ballroom was fifty feet long, there were a great many boughs to place. They chatted as they worked.

'Am I imagining things, or is Nick in the sulks?' Pel asked. 'I think he would have liked to help us do these decorations.'

'He is a little upset that Aurelia went off to Brighton without him, I believe.'

'Gudgeon. He ought to have gone with her. I ain't too sharp at picking up on affairs of the heart, but it seems to me Willie and Aurelia were looking pretty cozy at dinner. When the syllabub was served, she looked at Willie in a certain way, sort of moonish, and said, "We had this for luncheon." I don't know. As I say, I ain't too sharp, but I could have sworn she was flirting with him.'

'What did Willie say?'

'Nothing. That's just the point. He looked at his syllabub and turned pink as a rose. Now, why should a dish of syllabub make him blush? I've never seen Willie Winston blush before in my life, and I have known him from the egg.'

He placed the bough and they continued on to the next hook. 'It probably has something to do with meeting the prince,' Jane said. 'She is very excited about that.'

'And there's the fan.'

'I noticed she carried a fan. One does not often see ladies use them in winter. What has the fan to do with it?'

'I don't know that either, but every time she touched it, she looked at Willie in that way I was telling you about. Mushy.'

'I didn't notice anything.'

'You wasn't sitting across from her. I was. There was a noticeable breeze in that dining room. No wonder we are all catching cold, but she kept fanning herself between courses. Dashed odd.'

He peered into the hallway and put a finger to his lips. 'There is Willie back downstairs. He is supposed to be with Goderich.'

'I expect Goderich has fallen asleep by now.'

'And here comes Aurelia, darting out of the saloon to meet him. By the living jingo, I am right. There *is* something afoot between those two.'

'She is arranging some surprise for Nick. The only thing she brought back from Brighton was a bonnet. That cannot be the surprise.'

'You're right there. Her buying another bonnet is no surprise. Nick will have to set aside a special room to hold them.'

'Perhaps Willie is in on it and they are discussing it.'

Pel went closer to the door, drew it nearly shut to hide himself, and listened.

'Pelham Vickers!' Jane said in a condemnatory whisper. 'Don't eavesdrop! That is horrid.'

He made a shushing motion with his hand and applied his eye to the slit in the door.

He saw Aurelia vigorously fanning herself, and looking at Willie again in that mushy way. 'Willie,' she said softly.

'Where is Nick?' Willie asked, looking over his shoulder.

Pel beckoned Jane to the doorway. 'Listen to this!' he whispered excitedly. She only hesitated a moment before joining him. She felt like a criminal, but was too overcome with human curiosity to resist.

'He went to the library to get me a book,' Aurelia said. 'I told him I wanted one when I saw you come downstairs.'

'Sly minx!' Willie said approvingly. 'I see you are using your fan.'

Pel narrowed his eyes and bobbed his head at Jane, as if to say, *I told you so!*

'I shall always treasure it, Willie,' Aurelia said. 'This has been the most beautiful day of my whole life.'

'It is not every day one meets the prince,' he said, in a questioning way.

'It was not just meeting the prince,' she said, gazing at him and batting her eyelashes shamelessly.

'He's coming!' Willie cautioned, and they stepped apart. Aurelia hid the fan in the folds of her skirt and turned to greet Nick.

'We don't seem to have a copy of Byron in the library,' Nick said. 'I shall pick you one up in town. I am curious to have a look at his work myself.'

'Byron is best appreciated in person,' Willie said. 'His conversation outdoes even his poetry.'

'Do you know him, Willie?' Aurelia asked in an excited voice.

'Yes, I met him at Gentleman Jackson's Boxing Parlor.'

'Did you hear that, Nick? Willie knows Lord Byron.' Then she turned to Willie. 'You know everybody,' she sighed.

'Only the fashionable fribbles,' Willie said. 'It is our Nicholas who is acquainted with the worthies. And now I shall leave you two lovebirds alone. I have some letters to write.' He strolled away, and Nick led Aurelia back to the saloon.

'There you are,' Pelham said to Jane. 'Willie is trying to beat Nick's time. I knew he could not resist the Townsend fortune.'

'They didn't really say much,' Jane said uncertainly. 'It was sly of Aurelia to have sent Nick off for a book to be alone with Willie, but all she actually said was that she had had a wonderful day. And Willie didn't say anything incriminating.'

'He's too cagey for that. You saw the way they were looking at each other. I feel it my duty to tell Nick.'

'Oh, no! You mustn't! Let me talk to Aurelia. You have a word with Willie. There is no need to worry Nick about it. I'm sure it is just a . . . a passing fancy. Any girl's head might be turned by Willie. He is a wicked flirt, but it doesn't mean anything. Aurelia has known him for some time, you know. He is a friend of her sister.'

'With friends like that, she don't need enemies.'

'Let us go on with the decorating.'

He moved the ladder to the doorway that led into the hall, then climbed up, and Jane handed him a bough, which he fastened onto the hook above the door.

'Is this one crooked?' he asked, jabbing at it.

'It's lopsided. One side is heavier than the other.'

'I'll have to step back. It's easier to tell from a distance.' She moved back a few paces. 'Yes, it tilts to the left.'

Not liking to climb any higher than necessary, Pel only went halfway up the ladder, and worked with his arms stretched high over his head.

'Stay there and tell me when I've got it. I'll have to climb higher and see if I can wedge the bough to hold it straight.'

He climbed cautiously, grasping the protruding top of the doorframe to steady him as the ladder was inclined to wobble without Jane to steady it. It slipped on the oaken floor and went sliding out from beneath him, landing on the floor with a loud clatter. He managed to hold on to the top of the doorjamb for a minute, but the sharp edge bit into his fingers, and he soon had to let go. The door was eight feet high. It was not a dangerous drop, but he landed on the ladder with the fir bough sitting on his head.

Jane hurried forward to help him. 'Did you hurt yourself?'

He pulled the branches apart and peered through the bough. 'I've given my knee a wrench. I fear I may have busted it.'

# Chapter Twelve

$\mathcal{N}$icholas and Aurelia came running from the saloon to see what had caused the racket. 'Good lord, Pel! Are you all right?' Nick asked, helping him up.

Pel yanked the branch from his head and tossed it aside. He put his weight cautiously on his twisted knee and winced, took a step and winced again, but was soon standing without too much pain.

'It ain't broken at least. Daresay I can do without a sawbones poking at me, but you will have to let someone else climb that ladder. I ain't tackling it again. Never did like heights. Told you so. There are only two more boughs to hang.'

When Jane began brushing off Pel's jacket and straightening his cravat in a wifely way, Nick felt a pronounced fit of pique.

'The footmen can finish the job,' Aurelia said.

'Hanging the festive boughs has always been done by the family,' Nick reminded her.

'Tradition,' Pel said, giving the bough a kick.

'I shall hang the boughs,' Nick said, rescuing the fallen one from Pel's wrath.

'You might fall and hurt yourself,' Aurelia objected. 'You wouldn't be able to stand up with me at our ball.'

'I daresay Willie would be happy to take his place,' Pel said, with a sly look at Aurelia. Aurelia's head turned sharply to the hallway, where she had spoken with Willie. She cast a questioning look at Pel, then seized her lower lip between her teeth and looked nervous, realizing she had been overheard.

'Let me help you into the saloon, Mr Vickers,' Aurelia said, and gave him her arm to limp along to the grate, where she batted her long eyelashes at him and talked away his suspicions.

'Willie has been like an uncle to me, you must know,' Aurelia said. 'We are on familiar terms. He runs quite tame at the Huddlestons'. We are preparing a little surprise for Nick tomorrow. That is why I wanted a private word with him. There is nothing else between us.'

Pel was not often privy to a pretty lady's confidences. He realized, when she gazed soulfully at him with her lustrous eyes, that he had judged her severely, and said, 'You must not think I held you to blame. Willie ought to know better than to be having clandestine meetings, but—'

'It was not like that, Mr Vickers. May I call you Pelham?'

'I don't see why not. Everyone does. Or Pel.'

'I just happened to spot Willie, and wanted a word with him. That's all. I hope you won't mention it to Nick.'

'Why the deuce should I? I don't want to spoil the surprise. What is it, by the by?'

'I have bought a new carpet for the saloon, and some pretty lamps, and a lovely vase. The room is so shabby.'

'Good Lord!' Pel said on a strangled gasp. 'That will certainly surprise him.'

'I'm sure he will be pleased. They are in very good taste. Willie helped me pick them out.'

'I'm not sure that was wise, Miss— Aurelia. A bit previous, if you see my meaning. Lizzie won't care for it.'

'But Nick is making changes in running the farm. Why should I not improve the house?'

'Because Goderich has gone crazy, and can't run the farm. Lizzie is still sane. The things you bought – a wedding gift from your papa, are they?' he asked, trying to make sense of it.

'In a way. I am having the bills sent to Papa. He would not want me to be living in such a shabby old house.'

'I wouldn't mention about the shabby house. Just be sure you tell Lizzie the things are a wedding gift from your papa.'

'But I want them installed before the wedding. In fact, before my family arrives.'

'I could do with a glass of wine. A large glass,' Pel said. He couldn't think on a clear head. He would consult with Jane on this touchy matter. It was beginning to look as if Willie was up to one of his clever tricks, stirring up trouble for the innocent young bride. Lizzie would hit the roof if Miss Aurelia began rearranging the house while she was still its mistress. A dashed insult really.

In the ballroom, Jane held the ladder while Nick hung the few remaining boughs.

'You will be happy to hear I have apologized to Aurelia,' he said. 'Tomorrow morning I shall take the day off and take her to call on a few of our worthy neighbors. I have not been paying enough attention to her. In my eagerness to take hold of the reins of Clareview, I have left her too much to her own devices.'

'I am glad to hear you are coming to your senses,' Jane said. If

Aurelia had turned to Willie to ease her boredom, then Nick's company should bring the little flirtation to an end.

'And in the afternoon the Huddlestons arrive, so that should keep her happy.'

Jane thought it an odd thing to say, that Aurelia should prefer any company to her fiancé's. 'She is very close to her sister Marie, I believe. She speaks of her a great deal.'

'They are bosom bows. Mrs Townsend does not interest herself in social matters. It is Marie who is in charge of that. She has been her young sister's mentor since Aurelia went to stay with her in London.'

'Do you know the Huddlestons well?'

'Fairly well. Horace hasn't much to say for himself, but Marie is a lively lady. No nonsense about her. It was she who suggested Aurelia should accompany me home for Christmas.'

'I see.'

It occurred to Jane that the no-nonsense Marie might have engineered the engagement, as well as the visit. A wealthy cit, eager to make her way in society . . . Was it possible Aurelia was not in love with Nick? No, it could not be that. She had seemed quite simply infatuated with her fiancé when they first arrived at Clareview.

When the last bough was hung, Nick sat on top of the ladder and looked around the room with quiet satisfaction. Aurelia had been very understanding when he apologized for not going to Brighton with her. She was a sweet, biddable girl. It was only a last-minute jitters that troubled him about this marriage. No one had held a gun to his head. He loved Aurelia. She would soon settle into country ways and make an excellent wife.

'She really is very pretty, is she not?' he said.

'The prince had the right word for her. You and she will have wonderful children.'

'Yes, if they get her looks and my—' He came to an abrupt halt.

'Your tact? Your modesty? Your sensitivity?' she asked, with a laughing look. 'You have not been behaving very well, Nick.'

'I know it. I thought things would be different when I got home. More peaceful, or ... I don't know. Perhaps it is just Uncle's condition that keeps reminding me of death. I wanted to forget all about death.'

'Did you see very much of it?' she asked.

'Enough to last several lifetimes. It was seeing the youngsters blown to bits that was the hardest to take. And the courage, the bravery of them!' Jane got him, by a few leading questions, to tell her a little of his experiences. She could hardly believe the stories he told, yet the agony on his face when he spoke of these horrors was proof that he had witnessed them, and was forever changed by the experience.

'I shouldn't be talking to you of these matters. They aren't fit tales for a lady. I just wanted to come home and *"cultiver mon jardin,"* as Voltaire said. Yet I feel somewhat relieved for having shared it with you.'

'I would like to hear more sometime, but I fear only in small doses.'

He realized that he had never discussed these matters with Aurelia, nor had she been curious enough to ask. He had not spoken of them to anyone. They sat in his heart like a dark secret, forever a part of his memory. Why had he unburdened himself to Jane? Perhaps because she was the only one who cared enough to ask.

They went to the saloon, where they were soon joined by Lizzie and Willie for tea.

'I notice your silver teapot is dented, Aunt Lizzie,' Aurelia said.

'Yes, tradition has it that it occurred when a servant spilled tea on Marlborough – in Queen Anne's day, you know. Marlborough, in a fit of temper, swatted the pot out of the servant's hand.'

'Could the dent not be removed? Marie knows a silversmith in London who does that sort of work.'

Lizzie blinked in astonishment. 'Oh, my dear! I would not have the dent removed for worlds. This tea service is famous.'

'Was it the spilt tea that ruined the carpet?' Aurelia asked, staring at a stain on the old Persian carpet.

'Actually, Goderich did that. It is a wine stain. It might be removed, I daresay. He got totally disguised when he learned Prinny had married Mrs Fitzherbert. He was rather fond of Marie himself.'

Aurelia gave a commiserating smile for the lady's ignorance. 'You must be mistaken, Aunt Lizzie. The prince is married to Princess Caroline.'

'This was an earlier wedding. Quite irregular. It is the style to deny it ever occurred, I believe.'

Aurelia felt this sort of talk was bordering on the seditious, and changed the subject. She would ask the Huddlestons for a new tea service for a wedding gift. She was not going to serve tea from an old dented pot just because some hotheaded neighbor had lost his temper.

Before retiring, Nick and Aurelia took Lizzie to view the decorations in the ballroom. Willie tagged along. Pelham stayed behind with Jane.

'About Willie and Aurelia,' he said. 'I spoke to her. All a hum. They were talking about a surprise she is arranging for Nick. She's refurnishing Lizzie's saloon. The goods are to arrive tomorrow.'

'Without consulting Lady Elizabeth?' Jane asked, staring in disbelief.

'Or Nick. I see a spot of trouble rearing its head.'

'Oh dear! We cannot let this happen. Nick will be furious.'

'I believe I've come up with something. Letting on the stuff is a wedding present from Townsend. Do you think it will fadge? I fear it will have to. No time to cancel the orders. The goods are to arrive tomorrow morning.'

'You are a genius, Pel!'

'Oh, I wouldn't say that. I have been in a spot of trouble from time to time. A fellow learns how to lie, or give the truth a twist or two at least. Willie will want watching.'

'You think he is behind this?' Her knowing look told Pel she required no explanation as to why Willie should involve himself.

'I shouldn't be surprised. He has caught the scent of gold, and the aroma that Aurelia and Nick don't suit so well as they ought.'

'You feel that, too?' He gave her a sharp look. 'What . . . what I meant to say was, do you feel that way?'

'You were right the first time. I feel that way, too. We must be on our toes to keep this match from falling apart.'

Jane was disappointed at his conclusion. She soon learned the reason for Pel's concern. 'The girl is madly in love with Nick,' he said. 'She will soon catch on to how to please him. Meanwhile, we shall give her a little prod when she goes amiss. The least we can do for Nick. I know you want him to be happy as much as I do.'

'Oh yes, certainly.'

'Then it is settled. You keep an eye on her, and I shall watch out for Willie. Is it a bargain?' he asked, stretching out his hand.

'A bargain,' she said, taking his hand and giving it a firm shake.

They neither of them looked forward to the morrow with much pleasure.

# Chapter Thirteen

In the morning Nicholas took Aurelia, wearing her new bonnet, to call on some of his neighbors. The purchases from Brighton arrived during her absence. Jane and Pelham were prepared for a patch of stormy weather when Lizzie saw the roll of carpet coming in, but it was no such a thing. The wily Willie had had a word with her.

'Her papa gave her a couple of thousand to buy some gewgaws for her trousseau,' he had explained over breakfast. 'Rather than fritter away the money on bonnets and gowns, I suggested she invest in a few good pieces for Clareview. I know you are fond of Meissen, Aunt Lizzie. I think you will like the lamps I directed her to. They will brighten up a corner of your saloon. The carpet is also nice. If, at some future date, you decide to remove to the Dower House, you can take the spare carpet and lamps that the new ones replace.'

'You are up to all the rigs, Willie!' Lizzie said, laughing in approval. 'If she has any more blunt to squander, let her buy a new silver tea service, and I shall take the dented Queen Anne set to the Dower House.'

'If you don't, she will have the dent removed,' Willie replied, in the same jovial spirit.

'She really is incorrigible, but Nick don't seem to mind, so why should we?'

It was not Willie's intention to gain total approval of the match. He said, 'Why indeed? The only difficulty I foresee is that she doesn't care for the country. A pity. She will end up luring Nick off to London.'

Lizzie looked sharp at this. 'We can't have that! Why, Nick has spoken of nothing but how happy he is to be home. And really, you know, Fogarty has not been able to keep things up as he ought, what with Goderich forever pestering him about the donkeys.'

'Perhaps if she has plenty of visitors to keep her occupied here . . . Her family is a close one. They will spend a deal of time at Clareview, I expect.'

'Even an invasion of brewers would be better than her taking Nick off to London.'

When the parcels arrived from Brighton, Lizzie was the first one into the entrance hall to welcome them.

'Ah, the wedding gifts! Let us unwrap the carpet. I am dying to see it. We shall roll it back up again before she returns,' Lizzie said happily.

The carpet, an Aubusson in muted shades of rose and blue and black, was acceptable.

'My ruse worked pretty well, eh?' Pel said aside to Jane.

'Better than I thought.'

All the gifts proved to be in the best of taste. When Nick and Aurelia returned, they were smiling and laughing together.

'Oh, they have come!' Aurelia exclaimed. 'Come and see the surprise, Nick.'

Anyone can recognize a carpet, even before it is unrolled. Nick's eyes flew in alarm to his Aunt Lizzie. When he saw her complacent mood, he relaxed and praised the wedding gifts along with the others.

Over lunch, Nick and Aurelia discussed their visits. The bride-to-be, hot from Brighton and the prince's benediction, had proved a stunning success. Jane told herself she should be happy, but some corner of her heart was unconvinced. Nick was happy enough with Aurelia now, but would she prove suitable when the first bloom was off the rose of romance? She noticed that Nick's eyes glazed over when Aurelia told for the third time how Mrs Mandelson had reacted to the tale of the prince and the Incomparable.

'The prince always had an eye for an Incomparable,' Mrs Mandelson had said. 'I wager you reminded him of his first flirt, Mrs Robinson, you know, who played the role of Perdita in a play. You want to watch him, Colonel Morgan, or the prince will try to steal your bride away.'

'Perdita and Florizel, they used to call Prinny and his actress friend,' Lizzie said. 'My, how it takes me back. And Prinny is still legging it after the gels. Amazing stamina for one in his bloated condition. I hear he is fat as a flawn.'

After luncheon, Aurelia went abovestairs to have a look at the set of chambers chosen for the Huddlestons. She was not impressed with the heavy furnishings from the last century and a Rubens painting of a lady apparently being kidnapped by satyrs, but at least the window hangings were not faded, and the carpet still had some semblance of nap on it.

She had barely time to make a fresh toilette before the door knocker sounded, and a bustle belowstairs told her that Marie and Horace had arrived. When Jane first cast an eye on Mrs Huddleston, she had a strange feeling that time had raced forward a decade and a half, and she was looking at an older Aurelia, a sort of caricature of beauty gone wrong. It was the same sort of face, with the same blonde hair, but the softness of youth had hardened to arrogance. Lines from nose to chin had formed, and the flesh around the chin had begun to sag. The figure, encased in a smartly vulgar suit of scarlet, had filled out to matronly proportions.

Mr Huddleston, a quiet, well-behaved man, wore the slightly cowering air of resignation. He was tall and thin, with brown hair just turning silver at the temples. He answered when spoken to, and did just as his wife told him.

Introductions were made, coats and bonnets removed, and the guests were taken into the Gold Saloon.

'So this is Clareview,' Mrs Huddleston said, peering around the lofty chamber. The molded ceilings, the stretching length of the grand room, with half a dozen graceful windows looking out on a park, made her feel she was in a palace. She had decided, however, and informed her spouse, that they would not be impressed by Clareview. To praise it too much would give 'the in-laws,' as she called anyone connected to Nick, the notion that they had never set foot in a stately home before. 'It will cost you a fortune to heat this place, 'Relia,' she said.

'That is no problem, Mrs Huddleston,' Lizzie said. 'The wood comes from our own forest.'

Horace had mentioned that all the land they had been driving through for the last half hour belonged to Clareview. To a lady bred in the city, it seemed incredible that one family could own miles of land.

'Wood?' she asked. 'Good gracious, you ought to switch to coal. No one in London is using wood nowadays. It has been put out to pasture.'

'Not in the country,' Lizzie said. 'Would you care for some tea, Mrs Huddleston? After that long, chilly drive—'

'Chilly? Our carriage is as warm as toast. We have the best carriage that money can buy. I could do with a cup of tea, however. Horace would like one, too, wouldn't you, Horace?'

'That would be dandy,' Horace replied, and tea was called for.

Mrs Huddleston's sharp eyes did not overlook the dented teapot, nor did she hesitate to call attention to it, in what she considered a discreet way.

'I see what Horace and I will give you for a wedding gift, 'Relia,' she said playfully.

'As I was telling your sister yesterday, Mrs Huddleston,' Lizzie said, 'it was the Duke of Marlborough who caused the dent in this teapot.'

'You would think a duke would know better. I know just how it is. My neighbor, Mrs Empey, brushed against a table and knocked a vase of flowers onto the floor. The vase – a very nice crystal one – was smashed to smithereens, and she never even offered to pay for it.' When her story was met with a stunned silence, she was well satisfied. It left her free to hold center stage, her favorite spot.

'Well, Nick, so this is what you call home. I don't believe I have got all your relatives sorted out yet. Just who are you, exactly?' she asked, with a searching look at Jane.

'This is a neighbor and friend, Miss Ramsey,' Nick said. 'She is spending the Christmas holiday with us.'

'Friend of whom? Sly dog! We have caught you dead to rights

there, Nick. I would not let Horace have such a pretty neighbor move in, bag and baggage, on us. Just funning, Miss Ramsey. I can see you are no threat to 'Relia.'

Jane smiled weakly. Glancing at Nick, she saw he wore an air of embarrassment.

'Jane – Miss Ramsey's aunt is abovestairs. She has caught the cold that is going around,' Lizzie said.

'Dear me! And you already have old Goderich bedridden on your hands as well. You are turning the place into a regular nursing home, Lady Elizabeth. I hope Horace and I don't come down with it before 'Relia's ball. You had best move your chair closer to that bit of a fire, Horace. There is a wicked draft in here.'

It was not long before Mrs Huddleston had turned the conversation into the troubled water of the wedding and honeymoon.

'I have been in touch with St. George's to arrange the wedding for you, 'Relia,' she said. 'They are amazingly busy for the middle of winter. You have a choice of January seventeenth at ten o'clock in the morning – which is too soon. Mrs Stevenson cannot have your trousseau ready that early. The next free Saturday – you recall Papa particularly wants a Saturday date, so that he will be free – the next free Saturday is not until February.' She turned a playful eye on Nick. 'Do you think you can behave yourself that long, Nick? I shall take 'Relia back to London with me, of course. I expect you will be joining us pretty soon as well. You will want to get your mansion on Grosvenor Square opened up, and the servants hired, and so on before February the fourteenth.'

Aurelia cast a shy look at Nick. 'Is February the fourteenth all right with you, Nick?'

'We can always be married from Clareview, if that date is too long for me to keep myself in check,' he said, with a sharp look at Mrs Huddleston.

'Oh, no! We cannot ask all our guests to be trekking into the wilds in the wintertime, Nick,' Mrs Huddleston said. 'There is no counting on the weather. Besides, I have already booked the church for February the fourteenth, before someone beat us to it. Valentine's Day, you see. So appropriate. We will have some sort of hearts and lace and flowers as the theme for the wedding breakfast.'

'Won't that be sweet, Nick,' Aurelia said, smiling softly.

'I have not had time to look into the packets for Calais,' Mrs Huddleston continued unchecked. 'For the treacle moon, you know,' she added. 'Won't Wellington be surprised to see you land in on him. Horace can make those traveling arrangements for you, if you will tell us how many servants you plan to take with you.'

'Very kind, Marie,' Nick said, 'but we will not be going to Paris until the spring.'

'The spring? Why, there is no saying 'Relia will be in shape to travel by spring. Papa expects another grandson before the year is out, you must know. You want to take care of that as soon as possible in case anything should happen to you, Nick. You don't want Clareview falling into the hands of some yahoo.'

'Actually, my cousin Clarence Morgan would inherit the title and estate if I should die without issue. He is not a yahoo.'

'He's a vicar,' Pelham said, for he felt he ought to contribute something to the conversation.

Willie was amazingly quiet as he sat with a very satisfied smile, listening.

'Good God, a vicar!' Mrs Huddleston exclaimed. 'I see you

fine lords have your poor relations, the same as the rest of us. Would you mind just topping off this tea, Lady Elizabeth? How is yours, Horace? Mine has grown ice-cold from the drafts. You really should think of switching to coal, Nick.'

'I ain't poor!' Pelham said, but no one listened to him.

Lady Elizabeth poured more tea for them all, and the cakes were passed again. She wanted to give the woman a good setdown. *Her* relatives could not travel in winter, but Nick's could make the trip to London. She was so overwhelmed, she couldn't think of a thing to say.

Nick felt exactly the same way. He couldn't account for the change in Marie. In London she had seemed more agreeable. He had not spent much time in her company, but he had taken dinner with her and Horace a few times. She had been a bustling, busy sort of woman. He had thought perhaps it was nervousness at having a dinner party that caused it. Other than that, he had only seen her for a few moments when calling on Aurelia. Marie had suggested outings for them. As he thought back, he remembered that she had been pretty insistent that he take Aurelia to a certain play and had urged him more than once to remove from the hotel into the mansion on Grosvenor Square. But she had not tried to take over his whole life, as she was doing now.

'How is old Goderich anyway?' Mrs Huddleston asked, turning to Lady Elizabeth. 'Is it safe to go and have a look at him?'

'He enjoys company. I'm sure he would like to meet Aurelia's sister,' Lady Elizabeth replied, just managing to hang on to her temper. 'Have a look at him' indeed, as if he were a wild animal, or a freak.

'A pity he is hanging on so long. He must be a great trial to you, Lady Elizabeth. If he passed away soon, Nick could get married as Lord Goderich. That would look pretty fine in the journals, eh? I really don't see why you don't call yourself Lord Wyecliffe, Nick. There is no danger of Goderich's recovering, is there?'

'We have every hope for his recovery,' Nick said. Mrs Huddleston stared at him as if he had run mad.

'There is a marked improvement in his condition. In fact, he tells me he plans to attend the little New Year's party we are planning.'

'I suppose you could get away with it at a family party. As long as he doesn't come to the ball!' Mrs Huddleston said.

'We are not having a ball,' Lady Elizabeth said firmly. 'We are having a little New Year's party to celebrate Nick and Aurelia's engagement.'

'I see.' Mrs Huddleston turned a cool eye on her husband and said in a low voice, 'What a take-in! Dragging us all the way from London for a little party.'

Aurelia saw that her sister was offended and wanted a few moments of privacy with her. She suggested that the Huddlestons might like to go to their room and rest after the trip. Mrs Huddleston thanked her, and said that Horace was feeling a bit peaky. They would be down for dinner at eight.

'We keep country hours. Dinner is at six-thirty,' Lady Elizabeth said.

'Six-thirty! Why, that is the middle of the afternoon. If I had known that, I would not have eaten that second piece of plum cake. It was not at all bad, by the by, though I prefer currants to raisins myself. You must give me your cook's receipt, Lady Elizabeth.'

On this condescending speech, she herded Aurelia and Horace upstairs.

Nick was uncomfortably aware that all eyes were on him. While his inclination was to light into Mrs Huddleston with the rest of them, his duty was to defend his fiancée and her family. But what defense was possible?

'I shan't let Marie run Aurelia after we are married,' he said, and felt it was a totally inadequate defense. 'She has been *in loco parentis* to her sister since Aurelia's remove to London, and takes a close interest in her welfare, her wedding, and so on. It is only natural.'

No one said a word. They just looked at him in mute sympathy. Regret was transformed to anger as the enormity of his folly washed over him. Like Jane, he had noticed Marie's resemblance to Aurelia, and found himself imagining her in fifteen years. And himself, a Mr Huddleston.

Before he should say, or do, something rash, he rose. 'I am going upstairs. I shall be down for dinner. I have a slight megrim.'

'No wonder,' Lizzie said, once he was beyond earshot. 'Is there nothing we can do? Willie, you know these people. What do you think? What would it take to get rid of them?'

'I think Mrs Huddleston wants a noble connection and would not let Aurelia break off the match if she wanted to.'

'I could have crowned her when she said she wanted to "have a look" at Goderich, as if he were a raree-show. As to wishing he were dead so that the journals could trumpet Aurelia's marriage to a lord! I hope Goderich lives a good long time, to spite her.'

'What might change Marie's mind,' Willie said, with a cunning smile, 'is if we could convince her that Goderich is not only recovering, but planning to marry.'

'Nick would still be his heir,' Lizzie said.

'Not if Goderich had a son.'

'Good God! But it would never work. And who could he possibly marry? Not that I mean actually marry, but just to put her nose out of joint?'

'Mrs Lipton, perhaps,' Willie suggested. 'She is still young enough—'

'This is horrid!' Jane said, scowling at them. 'We should be thinking of ways to help Nick, not—'

'My dear girl,' Willie said. 'That is precisely what we are trying to do. You cannot imagine he still loves Aurelia. I swear he was gritting his teeth at luncheon when she told us for the third or fourth time how the prince is in love with her. We would be doing him a favor.'

'True,' Pel said. 'And if Willie's wrong, nothing we say or do could turn Nick from his path in any case, so where is the harm?'

'Well, I won't be a party to it,' Jane said, and left the room.

# Chapter Fourteen

**M**rs Huddleston did not improve on closer acquaintance, nor did Aurelia improve with her mentor to guide her in her approaching role as mistress of Clareview. Mrs Huddleston's public complaints and suggestions were couched in an arch manner to show her good humor, but there was a razor edge to them all.

'Should you not be sitting at the bottom of your fiancé's table, 'Relia, as Nick is sitting at its head?' she asked as they sat down to dinner that evening.

'Lady Elizabeth is our hostess,' Nick pointed out. 'She has asked me to take Uncle's place as host.'

''Relia is a little more than a guest, however,' Mrs Huddleston replied. Then she turned her steely gaze to Jane. 'Speaking of guests, how long did you say you planned to stay, Miss Ramsey?'

'I have been asked to remain until after the party – to help with the preparations, you know.'

'At home we had the servants do that sort of thing. I advise you do likewise in future, 'Relia. I am sure Miss Ramsey has a life of her own, beyond hanging around Clareview. You must be engaged, at your age, Miss Ramsey?'

'No, I am not,' Jane replied, concealing her discomfort as much as she could. 'I did not mean to stay so long, but my aunt caught a cold, you recall.'

'I noticed she was well enough to be dressed and sitting in old Goderich's bedchamber when I went abovestairs. I popped in to see him, by the by,' she added to Lady Elizabeth. 'I found him in better physical shape than I expected, but completely gaga. I could not make him understand who I was. He kept calling me Mrs Muldoon.'

A dreadful hush fell over the table. Mrs Muldoon was the publican's wife, a loud, vulgar, managing woman who served the tables at the local inn. Mrs Huddleston's similarity to this harpy was quite noticeable. Into the hush, Pel spoke.

'I see a likeness,' he said, studying Marie.

'Ah, and who is this Mrs Muldoon? A neighbor?'

Pel opened his mouth. Jane rushed in. 'Yes, she lives in Amberley.'

Mrs Huddleston nodded. 'As I said, his mind is gone completely. I am sure you could make some arrangement with your influential friends to assume the title of Lord Wyecliffe, Nick. Prinny might give you a hand, as he is so fond of 'Relia. There is no chance of old Goderich making a match.'

'I think not,' Nick said blandly. 'It is so common to be snatching at a title.'

Mrs Huddleston felt the sting in this speech. 'And so noble to be snatching at a fortune!' she riposted. She heard a sharp intake of breath from across the table. Willie, was it, or that Jane person? 'Not that I mean to say you are after Papa's money,' she added forgivingly. 'All the lads were dangling after 'Relia, even the ones with blunt of their own.'

148

'What do you hear from your sister, Marie?' Willie asked, to maintain some semblance of dignity at the dinner table.

Eleanor's doings – enceinte again – got them through the fish course. The affairs of Mr Townsend were so multifarious that he lasted through the next two courses, with a little diversion into London society by Willie when the going became rough.

After the worst meal of her whole life, Jane was glad to escape to the saloon while the gentlemen took their port. She was not anticipating the interval with the Townsend sisters with anything like pleasure, but at least Nick would not be there, writhing in embarrassment and biting his tongue to keep it in check. He must love Aurelia desperately to maintain a discreet silence in the face of that woman's provocation.

Mrs Huddleston did not accompany them to the saloon. She said to Lady Elizabeth, 'Nature calls. I must take a quick nip upstairs. I shan't be long,' then she darted upstairs and remained there, with a short stop en route to view 'Relia's Van Dycks, until the gentlemen joined the ladies.

When she returned below, she said in a carrying voice for all to hear, 'I sent your aunt back to bed, Miss Ramsey. She was tiring Goderich out. It is odd she did not join us for dinner, if she is well enough to be up and about, is it not?'

'She did not want to be coughing at the table,' Jane said. 'As Lord Goderich already has the cold, she feels she can visit with him.'

'I wager she caught it off of Goderich. Not wanting to be coughing on us is *one* explanation for her absence,' Mrs Huddleston said, with a sapient look.

Nick could take no more. 'Have you a more likely one, Mrs Huddleston?' he asked stiffly.

'I would like a word with you in private, Nick,' she replied. That cold 'Mrs Huddleston,' when she was accustomed to being called 'Marie,' was a warning to her. She had got on a first-name basis with Nick on his second visit to Upper Grosvenor Square. 'No hurry. We shall discuss it later. Now, what shall we do to amuse ourselves? The evening is so long when you take dinner in the middle of the afternoon.'

'Would you like a few hands of whist?' Lady Elizabeth suggested.

'Why not? We have enough for two tables. We'll put the youngsters at one table. Willie, you must make up the fourth at ours, along with Horace and myself and Lady Elizabeth. You can partner Nick, 'Relia, and give Miss Ramsey a chance with Mr Vickers.' She gave Jane a winking nod, as if to say, *a chance to nab him, slow top.*

'I don't like cards,' Aurelia said.

'No more do I,' her sister said, 'but we can hardly sit here staring at each other all evening.'

In fact, she did enjoy cards, and was good at the game. With the wily Willie as her partner, she made a tidy sum, which did not deter her from keeping a sharp eye on the other table, where she noticed Aurelia sat listlessly, while the cunning Miss Ramsey flirted with the gentlemen.

Horace's frequent refilling of his wineglass soon had him nodding. After an hour, the game broke up.

'Go to bed. Horace. I'll see you in your study now, Nick, if you are free,' Mrs Huddleston said, and strode from the room. She had already toured the house and discovered the location of the study.

Nick refused to become a second Horace and remained behind

a few moments, pouring wine and chatting unconcernedly, while trying to get his temper in check.

'Marie is waiting for you, Nick,' Aurelia reminded him after a moment.

Just as he opened his lips to give a setdown, Jane said, 'I shall look after Aurelia, Nick. You can go ahead.'

He glared, and left. Mrs Huddleston sat in his uncle's chair behind the oak desk. 'Sit down,' she said, in the tone of invitation.

'I would prefer to stand. What is it, Marie?'

She rose, shut the door, and stood facing him. 'It is that Mrs Lipton woman,' she said.

'Surely you mean lady?'

'Call her what you like, she is dangling after your uncle. It is all a plot, lad, and you are too innocent to see it. She cannot be a day over forty, and plenty young enough to land a son in over your head to diddle you out of the title and estate.'

'What if she does? I have an estate of my own bordering on Clareview.'

'A piddling seven hundred acres, and what is it – five thousand a year? You represented yourself as the heir to Clareview, and a great bosom bow of Wellington's. Now you are digging in your heels against going to Paris. If you have neither the title nor the wits to make a career for yourself through your influential friends, what will become of you?'

'I can make a good living from my own estate.'

'And a retired officer's half pay,' she said ironically. 'That would not keep 'Relia in bonnets.'

'Aurelia has sufficient bonnets to last a lifetime.'

'I believe you are as crazy as your uncle. I give you fair warning, Nick, you either take this situation in hand, or I shall advise Aurelia to jilt you.'

'And do you think she will do as you say?' he asked, in a silken voice.

Her lips clenched into a harsh line for a moment. Then she opened them and said bluntly, 'No, I don't. There is the mischief in it. Now, let us talk like sensible people. You claim to love Aurelia. Naturally I believe you, for everyone loves her. Think of her, not yourself. Do you want to bury that innocent child in the sticks, on a farm of seven hundred acres? Why, you and she could be the toast of London. A prime ministership is not beyond you in the future, if you play your cards right. Will you do as I ask?'

He looked at her in a puzzling way, not replying.

'Will you do what is best for Aurelia?' she asked grimly.

'Yes, I will, Marie,' he said. 'And I thank you for your advice.'

She smiled in triumph. 'No hard feelings. It is my custom to say what is on my mind. Perhaps my wits have been sharpened from association with Papa. There is no grass growing under his feet. He did not rise from the dirt to become the second largest brewer in England by being foolish. Naturally you have not had my opportunities to look out for yourself. You had it all handed to you on a silver platter. I shall be right there by your side to steer you straight if you begin to wander, after you remove to London. I am glad we had this little talk. I understand you cannot turn the Lipton woman off when she claims to be ill, but you must keep her away from Goderich. I wager she is up there now, sweet-talking the old goat.'

'I shall go abovestairs at once and look into it,' he said.

'I knew I might count on you. You're not quite as sharp as Willie, but you'll do.'

She gave his arm a sharp squeeze and they left the study. Nick went abovestairs, where he found his uncle being entertained by his valet, Rogers.

'How are you tonight, Uncle?' Nick asked.

'Never felt better. It is good having the house full of young ladies again.'

'You would have better luck with them if you shaved off that beard and had your hair cut.'

'I know it. Jane tells me it would please her. We'll do it this minute if you will stay here to see Rogers don't cut my throat. Will you do it?'

'With the best will in the world. Get the scissors and razor, Rogers.'

Rogers gurgled his pleasure as he rushed off to prepare for this job he had been long urging on his master.

'You aren't forgetting the New Year's party, Uncle?' Nick said. 'Do you feel you are up to visiting it?'

'I will dance every dance!'

'Say . . . every second dance. We don't want to waltz you into an early grave.'

'Waltz – I cannot hope to master the waltz, but I would like to see it. They tell me you get to hold the girls in your arms. Shocking! I wish I could do it.'

Lord Goderich sat in a chair in the middle of the room with a towel over his shoulders while Rogers performed the haircut and shave, with Nick looking on. As the white hair fell to the floor, Nick wondered if he was taking the coward's way out. He had offered for Aurelia, after all, and been accepted. He remembered Wellington's advice during a skirmish between Ciudad Rodrigo and Salamanca, when they had to make a temporary retreat.

'The men will think we're cowards!' Nick had objected.

'Better cowards for a day than dead for the rest of our lives,' Wellington had said. 'Some odds are best turned down, Colonel. There is such a thing as horse sense.'

Whatever about the morality of it, the improvement in his uncle's spirits was surely a good thing. Goderich looked a decade younger when the job was finished.

When he went to the mirror to view himself, his step was steadier. He looked in the mirror and said, 'Good God, who is that ugly old man? I look like my grandfather.'

'A fine old gentleman, your grandpapa,' Rogers said fondly.

'Aye, he had bottom. Still riding to hounds when he was my age. Bring my jacket, Rogers. Let me see if I can hold up the shoulders.'

He put the jacket on over his nightgown. It hung loosely, but not so loosely as to appear ludicrous. He straightened his shoulders and pulled in his stomach.

'I would like to learn the waltz,' he said. 'Show me how it goes, Nick.'

'For that, we will require music – and a lady.'

'Rogers will play his recorder for us. Do you know any waltzes, Rogers?'

'Indeed I do,' Rogers said, and darted off to bring his flute.

'And the lady?' Nick said.

Even before thinking of Aurelia, he thought of Jane. Aurelia disliked visiting his uncle in any case. When Rogers returned, he told him to ask Jane to come upstairs for a moment.

Jane went willingly enough. She assumed her aunt wanted something, and felt guilty at having deserted her for so long.

'It is Lord Goderich,' Rogers explained as they went upstairs.

'I hope he has not taken a turn for the worse?'

'No, for the better,' Rogers said merrily. 'He wants to see a waltz performed.'

'I didn't realize he had ever heard of the waltz.'

'Oh, I try to keep him informed what is afoot in the world, Miss Ramsey.'

She was surprised to see Nick in Goderich's room when she entered. 'You should have brought Miss Townsend up,' she said to Rogers.

'Colonel Morgan wanted you.'

Her eyes flew to Nick's, to see the laughter lurking there. 'Well put, Rogers,' he said. 'The music, if you please.'

# Chapter Fifteen

Jane was still stinging from Mrs Huddleston's attack on her. If the harpy learned she had slipped away from the party for a private waltz with Nick, what would she not have to say? Jane's first anger was for Mrs Huddleston, then it grew to include Nick for his poor judgment in asking her up here, and worst of all, she was angry with herself for feeling a wild rush of heat that must be joy. *Colonel Morgan wanted you.* But he only wanted her to show Goderich the waltz. Let him waltz with Aurelia.

She turned to Nick in wrath. 'Are you mad?' she asked.

In the heat of anger, her eyes sparkled dangerously. Her hair glistened like new copper in the lamplight. Heightened emotion lent a rosy blush to her cheeks and a fire to her voice. She looked like a highly incensed Venus. Not a pale Botticelli, but a flamboyant Titian or Giorgione.

Nick just gazed a moment, then said, 'No, I rather think I am experiencing a belated bout of sanity. Come, Uncle wants to see the waltz.' He took her hand.

She wrenched her fingers free. 'Ask your fiancée,' she said, and strode from the room.

Nick rushed after her. 'Jane! Wait! We can't disappoint Goderich.'

'Ask Aurelia to waltz with you. Why me?'

'Because she won't come. She dislikes visiting Goderich. It is only a waltz,' he said persuasively.

'You know what Mrs Huddleston will say.'

'Never mind Marie. What will Uncle think, if you refuse him this simple request? You didn't even look at him, or say good evening. He has made a special toilette to impress you.'

'What do you mean?'

'Come and see for yourself.'

He led a reluctant Jane back into the bedchamber. 'Oh, Lord Goderich!' she exclaimed, when she saw him all shaven and shorn, and wearing a jacket for the first time in years. 'I hardly recognized you! When did you – Who – My, don't you look fine!'

'By God!' he said, staring at her with the frank eye of childhood. 'You are a beauty. I wish I could stand up with you myself. Give an old man a treat and show me this new dance Rogers has been telling me about.'

She found refusal hard when he asked her pointblank. 'There is hardly room,' she said, looking about the chamber. Although it was spacious, it had the cluttered air a room takes on when it has become one's only living space. Extra tables had been brought in to hold the various items Goderich used to fill his long days. Medications, books, games, cards, a magnifying glass, two or three shawls; there was a comfortable upholstered chair by the window for reading, with a table beside it to hold tea or lunch. He had his collection of butterflies – three large framed racks – placed against the wall at the foot of his bed so he could look at them while in bed. It would take an age to clear the room.

Nick, not to be thwarted, said, 'Then we'll waltz in the hallway. It is plenty wide enough. Rogers, draw Uncle's chair up to the door so that he might see us.'

'That's the spirit that defeated Boney!' Goderich said, rubbing his hands in anticipation.

Jane still felt it was a rash thing to do, but she could not disappoint Lord Goderich. It had been a long time since she had seen him looking so happy. She examined the hallway, which was as wide as a small room, and realized she could not use its size as an excuse.

Rogers drew the chair to the doorway. Nick said to him, 'Let the music begin.' Then he bowed to Jane. 'Miss Ramsey, will you give me the pleasure of standing up with me?'

'I will be honored, sir,' she replied with a curtsy. They moved into the hallway, which stretched a clear fifty feet before turning a corner at either end. Rogers played his flute, which lent an eerie, plaintive air to the music. But when they began to waltz, she forgot all the odd circumstances of the dance and thought only of being in Nick's arms. They danced in a golden glow, tinged with regret, or nostalgia. For Jane, it was a bittersweet moment that made her realize just what she had missed when she lost Nick. No, not lost. She had never won him. The mood became so pervasive that she felt she must speak, to break the spell of his dark eyes, gazing at her.

'You must have learned to waltz since returning from Spain,' she said in a calm, social voice.

Nick just smiled enigmatically, as if enjoying a secret. It was a long, slow smile that seemed to look into her very heart. At length he said, 'Let us not spoil it with words, Jane. Words are

159

what do the mischief. Some things are best enjoyed by just doing them.'

They moved together in perfect rhythm down the long length of the hall, circling and wheeling as if they were one, each step anticipated. It was a waltz like no other Jane had ever experienced. Nick's arms tightened insensibly, until she could feel his strong chest pressing against her as they whirled up and down the hallway, past the gilt-framed ancestors on the wall, skirting the plant stands in front of the dark windows, past the grand staircase with the chandelier glowing like a magic waterfall of light below, oblivious to Lord Goderich, tapping his toe in time to the plaintive notes of the flute.

She wondered what were the words that Nick regretted. In this mood, she could almost imagine they were his offer to Aurelia. Surely he must feel this closeness, this sense of all being right with the world that was suffocating her. She wished the dance would never end, but all too soon the notes of the flute died, and they had to stop.

Nick held her hand tightly as they returned to Goderich's doorway. 'Thank you, Jane. You are a darling to oblige Uncle – and me. We shall do this again on New Year's.'

She bobbed a playful curtsy, knowing it would not be the same at a public party, with crowds milling about. The best part of it had been the privacy.

Goderich clapped his hands. 'That's a caution,' he said. 'I don't know how you do it without walking all over each other. The pair of you move like a well-matched team. Made for each other! You have chosen your bride wisely, Ronald. That publican's daughter is not the girl for you. What happened to her?'

Nick gave Jane a mischievous wink. 'I am glad you enjoyed it,

Uncle. And now we must let Rogers get you to bed, if you want to be in shape for the party on New Year's.'

'I wouldn't miss it, by gad. I just wish I were half a century younger and I would show you all the way. Good night, all. Thank you, my dear,' he said, taking Jane's hand and raising it to his lips, with a mischievous look at Nick.

'Beating my time, Uncle?' Nick asked.

'No, lad, time has beaten me, but I have a few licks in me yet.'

He went laughing into his room, and Nick led Jane to the staircase.

'I thought he was much better, until he called you Ronald,' Jane said. She felt it behooved her to ignore Goderich's notion that she was Nick's fiancée.

'What a discreet lady you are,' Nick said with a conspiratorial grin that told her he had read her mind.

'Does he really plan to attend the party?'

'Why not? It is his house. I, for one, should love to see him there.'

As they approached the bottom of the stairs, Jane cleared her throat nervously and said, 'Nick – about Mrs Huddleston. She will ask where we have been if we go into the saloon together. You go first.'

'Nonsense. We are a well-matched team, you and I. We shan't let her break us up. If she asks where we were, we shall tell her. We wouldn't want to lie.'

'You know what I mean,' she said with a *tsk*.

'Indeed I do. But you must know it is your aunt who has set her cap for Uncle. You are innocent in that respect. We have been saying good night to Uncle. *C'est tout.*'

'Aunt Emily setting her cap for Goderich? You cannot be serious! Did she say that?'

161

He gave a careless laugh, but with a touch of scorn to it. 'You and Mrs Lipton are such slow tops. You refuse to chase after a gentleman. That is no longer the way of the world. The times are changing, Jane, and we must change with them or be left behind. You are too nice – that is your problem. And before you tell me what my problem is, I suggest you say your good nights and retire to avoid the interrogation, if the prospect of it bothers you. You really ought to develop a temper to go with that red hair, you know.'

She thought perhaps all this was an oblique explanation of why he was marrying Aurelia. It was true the times were changing; many of the old aristocratic families were marrying into the newly rich merchant class. Nick's bride would not be the only lady who was unsure of her footing in society. Jane had read that this was a good thing. The possibility of social advancement prevented the sort of revolution France had experienced.

She was saved any embarrassment from Mrs Huddleston. That dame felt she had talked some sense into Nick and hardly glanced up when they entered. She had collared Willie and was sitting with him and Aurelia, discussing wedding plans, while Pel and Lady Elizabeth chatted quietly in a corner. Nick, Jane noticed, joined his aunt and Pel, after bowing to the others.

Jane said good night to everyone and made her escape without a single question. She went to say good night to Mrs Lipton, then retired to her own room in a strangely lethargic mood. She had felt, while dancing with Nick, that something might come of it, but his remarks afterwards told her he was satisfied with the status quo.

She missed the battle that soon ensued belowstairs. When Nick strolled over to the grate, Mrs Huddleston looked up sharply and said, 'So there you are! What were you and Miss Ramsey up to?'

'We were abovestairs with my uncle. I am happy to tell you he is wonderfully improved, and will definitely be attending our New Year's party.'

'You must be joking!' Mrs Huddleston exclaimed. 'He looks witless, with that hair streaming all over his face.'

'He has had his hair barbered, and his beard shaved off. He will attend the party.' He did not raise his voice, but there was an icy edge to it that his aunt, listening from her corner, recognized as spelling trouble.

She moved over to the grate to hear what was going forth, and lend Nick assistance if necessary. Willie said, 'You must not worry, Mrs Huddleston. Goderich will only stay a moment. He will have a glass of wine, flirt with a few ladies, and go back to his room.'

'But Papa is coming all the way from Manchester,' Mrs Huddleston said, bridling. 'I am the one who arranged this match. I have been telling him what a grand one it is for 'Relia. What will he think to see Goderich drooling into his collar, making a spectacle of himself in front of everyone? We will be laughing stocks. Tell him, Aurelia.'

Lady Elizabeth's lips stretched into a villainous smile. 'This decision is not for you and Aurelia to make, Mrs Huddleston. This is my brother's house,' she said. 'Naturally he will attend his own party if he wishes.' She turned to Aurelia. 'When you become the mistress of Clareview, you must learn to put our people first. Meanwhile, I am the hostess.'

'Not for long, old lady!' Mrs Huddleston said, girding up for battle.

'Well, well,' Willie said, smiling uncertainly. 'How quickly we have all become one ha – one big family. Here we are, squabbling amongst ourselves as if we had been kin forever. That is what happens when two strong personalities clash.' He turned a warning eye on Mrs Huddleston. 'But I fear you are in the wrong this time, Marie. Aunt Lizzie is right. The decision is hers to make. One never argues with one's hostess.'

Mrs Huddleston took Willie's word for law in social matters. She felt this insistence on dragging Goderich to the party was Nick's way of asserting his independence. Certainly she would have done no less, if she were in his position. And besides, everyone knew the aristocracy had some queer twists in them.

'Right, as usual, Willie,' she said, and added to Lady Elizabeth, 'We shall hold our noses in the air and give a good setdown to anyone who laughs at Goderich.'

'I am sure none of *my* friends would be so underbred,' Lady Elizabeth replied demurely, accepting the olive branch, but none too securely. 'And now would anyone like tea before retiring?'

'I would love a cup of tea, Lizzie,' Mrs Huddleston said, and the matter was closed. 'It seems so stiff to go on *lady*ing you when we have had our first little tiff.'

Aurelia turned to Nick and said, 'I won't have to stand up with your uncle, will I, Nick?'

'I doubt he will dance.'

'Good.'

The squabble seemed to have the effect of clearing the air. Mrs Huddleston became quite affable over the tea tray. There would be time to put Lady Elizabeth in her place after the wedding. Lady Elizabeth returned the affability – but she did not call Mrs Huddleston Marie, nor did she forget that stinging 'old lady.'

When the group dispersed some time later, Nick remained behind in the saloon with Pelham.

'I think you was pushing it a bit, Nick,' Pel said. 'Not like you to be so rough with the ladies. You used to handle such matters more tactfully.'

'I blame it on Spain,' Nick replied, with a remote smile.

'I daresay that's it. But these Spanish manners will lose you your bride, if you don't watch it.'

'I shall bear it in mind.'

'It's a rum thing, marriage, ain't it? I doubt I'm cut out for it.'

'I think you offered for Jane?' He listened closely for the answer.

'Not as you might say offered. I mentioned it. She didn't take me up on it. I am just as glad, to tell the truth. I am hoping she's forgotten. She's a nice girl, but I notice she's got a little streak of Huddleston in her.'

'*Jane?*' Nick exclaimed in astonishment.

'She's been nagging at me, Nick. Suggesting I go for walks, and stop drinking so much. Keeps at me to learn the wedding ceremony for you and Aurelia. She wants to change me.'

'I daresay if you don't mention marriage again, she will forget all about it.'

'I'm counting on it. Out of sight, out of mind – or out of hearing at least, if you know what I mean. A pity Aurelia wouldn't forget you offered for her, but her sister won't let her.' He peered to see how this hint went down.

After a moment, Nick said, 'Is it that obvious?'

'Only to me. Known you forever. That's it, then? You do want out?'

'Passionately.'

'Thought so. Good luck.' He peered around to see that Jane was not spying on him, then reached for the wine decanter.

An hour later, two fairly disguised gentlemen climbed the stairway to their beds.

# Chapter Sixteen

Mrs Huddleston, like her sister, was a devotee of shopping. No one, including Nick and certainly including Mr Huddleston, offered the least objection when she announced the next morning at breakfast that she would like to go to Amberley. Willie offered to take her. It is not to be imagined that Aurelia would miss out on the trip. At ten o'clock Mrs Huddleston's magnificent carriage and team of blood bays were brought from the stable. As she had no crest to bedizen her door panel, she had added a branch of hop leaves, which passed at a glance for ducal strawberry leaves. Intertwined amidst the foliage the words 'Townsend Brewery' in small gilt Gothic script, might be read by a very sharp-eyed reader. The footmen, all three of them, wore livery in the golden hues of Oldham Ale.

'I doubt we will be home for luncheon, Lizzie,' she announced upon leaving, and added less affably to her husband, 'Horace, you behave yourself while I am gone.'

Then she strode out, wearing a feathered bonnet so broad she could hardly get into the carriage, and a fur-lined cape with such lavish fox trim from collar to hem that it had denuded a dozen foxes.

'If you will steer me to the library, I will get out of your hair,' Horace said apologetically to his hostess.

No one knew whether his wife had told him of the altercation belowstairs the night before. His air of apology was even more pronounced than usual, but that might have been due to his having drunk too much the previous evening. He was directed to the library and did not appear again until luncheon.

Nick said, 'I am riding over to Milsham's farm this morning to have a look at his herd. I am exchanging two of our donkeys for a couple of his heifers. His children want a donkey cart.'

Jane said to Pelham, 'We shall go over the wedding service, Pelham.'

Pel gave a meaningful look to Nick, as if to say, *What did I tell you?* He cleared his throat and said, 'Actually, I have promised Nick I would go with him.'

He hadn't, but Nick seconded him in this untruth. 'Good. You can lead Miranda,' he said.

'Eh? Who the deuce is Miranda? Have the guests for the party begun arriving already?'

'Miranda is a donkey.'

'That is no way to speak of – Ah, just so. A real donkey. Let us go.'

Mrs Lipton had recovered sufficiently to rejoin the party. She had a deal to get caught up on, and passed a most enjoyable morning being informed of Mrs Huddleston's many vulgarities, as the ladies sat around the grate in Lizzie's private parlor, sewing.

'Nick would have done better to marry Jane after all,' Emily said, 'despite the money and tied houses.'

'The devil take the tied houses. They are nothing else but

168

taverns, Emily, where Townsend forces everyone to drink his ale. Did you hear what she said when she left? "I doubt I will be home for luncheon." What the devil does that mean? Will she be here or not? I'll be demmed if I will hold lunch for her. You must excuse my profanity, but really if I don't swear, I shall explode. I had no notion of letting Goderich come to the party, but he will be there now, if I have to have him hauled down on a litter. I am sorry Nick made him get a shave and a haircut. He looks nearly respectable.'

Jane already knew of Mrs Huddleston's behavior at first hand, which left her mind free to wander. Mostly it wandered to the long hallway abovestairs, where she relived again that magical waltz with Nick.

The Huddleston party did not return for luncheon. In fact, they were late for dinner. Amberley was so poorly able to fill Mrs Huddleston's needs that she had taken a dash to Brighton, and came sailing in the front door just as the dinner gong sounded. She was followed by three footmen, each loaded down with parcels. Willie was pressed into service as well, but his burden was light: only a bandbox.

'I see you are back,' Lizzie said, with a pointed look at the long-case clock. 'I shall ask Cook to hold dinner until you have had time to change, Mrs Huddleston.'

'I had forgotten you keep such odd hours,' Mrs Huddleston retorted, 'but you must not let us detain you. We shall not bother to change. We shall just remove our bonnets and pelisses and be with you as fast as a cat can lick its whiskers.'

Some twenty minutes passed before the bonnets and coats and pelisses were stowed, and Mrs Huddleston had done a quick count of bags and boxes to determine that none of her parcels had been left behind. The scurrying around left her coiffure so disheveled that she must dart abovestairs to give it a brushing.

'For I would not want to appear a savage in front of Lizzie,' she said, with an ingratiating smile.

'A little late for that,' Lizzie said in an undertone to Emily after the woman had departed.

Aurelia spoke to Nick while this was going forth. 'I am sorry we are so late, Nick. I told Marie from the beginning we might as well go to Brighton, but she wanted to see Amberley before we left. We might still have been home in time if she had not lingered so long by the prince's pavilion, hoping for a sight of him.'

'And did you see him?'

'No,' she said sadly. 'Oh, by the way, Marie says Norman's little church would not begin to hold all the people we are inviting to the wedding, so it seems we cannot be married there after all. She suggested that if you spoke to some archbishop or some such thing, he might allow Mr Vickers to marry us in London, if you have your heart quite set on your friend's marrying us.'

He was saved from replying by Willie, who came forward to join them and add his apologies for the lateness of their arrival.

'There was no dragging the ladies away from the shops,' he said. He looked so weary that Nick hadn't the heart to berate him.

Dinner was an uncomfortable meal, not the strained sort of discomfort wherein no one can think of anything to say, but the other sort, wherein the loudest talker allows no one else to get a word in edgewise. Mrs Huddleston's notion of conversation was to describe every item seen in the shops and reveal which of her acquaintances had a bonnet or lamp or chair just like it. These ladies were all unknown to everyone but the Huddlestons and

Aurelia. Marie's chatter did not prevent her from cleaning her plate, after first sniffing at every dish.

During the performance, Jane peered down the table to see if Aurelia was flirting with Willie. She could not see her, but she did observe the silk fan sitting by her plate. She also saw the expressions on various faces. Poor Horace Huddleston wore a look of utter tedium, occasionally varied by shame when his wife crossed the line from poor taste into outright vulgarity. She pitied Nick. This was his future she was looking at. Yet when she glanced at him, he seemed perfectly content. He was smiling. When he looked up and caught her eye, he lifted his glass in a silent toast, and drank. He didn't wink, but something in his look gave the same impression. It was the way his eyes sparkled mischievously and his lips moved unsteadily, as if trying not to laugh.

That look angered her. Here was she pitying him, and he hadn't even the wits to realize what he was getting himself into with this marriage. It must be true, then, that love was blind, and apparently deaf as well. Of course, none of this bothered Pelham. He ate his way stolidly through the two courses and removes, adding another few pounds to his ever-spreading girth. Strangely, it was Willie Winston who seemed disconcerted. It was he who winced when Marie poked her goose and said, 'A bit tough, is it not? I would have left it hanging a few more days if I were you, Lizzie.'

'I am so sorry, Mrs Huddleston,' Lady Elizabeth riposted. 'I was sure your jaws were up to anything.'

'Did I mention we ran into Cousin George in Brighton, Lizzie?' Willie said, and diverted any further exchange of fire between the ladies.

The meal lasted an hour, which seemed much longer, but eventually it was over and the ladies retired to the Gold Saloon, where Mrs Huddleston went to the sofa and began rooting about amongst her parcels, opening them to show the ladies her purchases.

'It looks as if this might take a long time,' Lizzie said, not without interest. Like any lady, she was curious to see what was in the parcels. 'Would you mind going up to sit with Goderich, Emily? He was asking for you in particular.'

Mrs Huddleston looked sharp at this, but eagerness to get into her bags and boxes prevented an argument.

'I would not tire the poor soul out, Mrs Lipton,' she said. 'Just see if he wants anything.'

'Oh, dear Emily never tires Goderich,' Lizzie said. 'Quite the contrary. Her visits have a most beneficial effect on him. We hold Mrs Lipton responsible for the improvement in his health.'

'Show them the lace, Marie,' Aurelia said, and Mrs Lipton escaped without further ado.

There was a great rustling around to find the lace. 'Now, which parcel is it in? Is it that gold box, 'Relia? No, that is the muff I got for Mama for the wedding. It was a bag, was it not? You remember I had to tell that stupid clerk to put paper between the layers. The blue bag, that's it. Hand it over, dear.'

She drew out a length of lovely blond lace from Belgium and held it up. 'What do you think of that, eh? That will go on 'Relia's wedding gown. It cost me a fortune, but of course, Papa has given me carte blanche to do the thing up in style. You need not fear I will land the bills in on Nick, Lizzie.'

The lace, a beautiful piece of work, was passed around and praised. Other items were also examined, until, as Lizzie told Emily Lipton later, 'the saloon looked like a drapery shop.'

172

That was precisely the effect when the gentlemen joined the ladies. Ells of silk and merino hung from the back of the sofa, with cards of buttons and ribbons everywhere. The ladies had so enjoyed their vicarious shopping spree that they had not noticed the time passing, but when Jane glanced at the clock, she saw it was nearly nine o'clock. The gentlemen were called to admire the haul from Brighton, glanced in confusion at the lace, fur muff, assorted ells of this and that, said, 'Very nice,' and promptly changed the subject.

'You don't think there might be money to be made from the donkeys?' Willie asked Nick.

'I don't intend to lose on them,' Nick replied. 'They are cheap enough to feed; they will eat anything, but they take up space. I am not interested in breeding them. I shall sell them off to anyone who will take them.'

'Ass's milk is valued by invalids, I believe,' Horace said.

His wife was reminded of her husband's existence by this speech, and told him he wanted to go to bed, but he might wait until the tea tray had come in.

'I expect you are waiting for Mrs Lipton to rejoin us,' she said to Lizzie. 'Surely it has not taken her this long to say good night to Goderich. Should you not send up to see if she is coming down again?'

'We shan't wait for Emily. She sometimes takes her tea with Goderich. They are such good friends,' she said, smiling placidly at Mrs Huddleston.

'Then what are we waiting for?' was the snappish reply. Of course, it was not an eagerness for her tea, but the possibility that Emily Lipton was inveigling herself into a ladyship that bothered her.

When the tea tray finally arrived, Marie took her cup and sat with Nicholas. 'If you are wise, you will send that Mrs Lipton packing,' she said, 'now that she is out of her bed.'

'I doubt Lord Goderich would permit it. She is his special guest, you must know. It is not for me to turf out his company.'

Jane, who sat with Pel, did not hear any of these *sotto voce* conversations. She saw only that her aunt was missing her tea, and went abovestairs to get her. As soon as she left the room, Nick also rose.

'Perhaps you are right,' he said to Mrs Huddleston. 'I shall ask Mrs Lipton to join us.'

'Now you are talking sense!'

He caught up to Jane at the top of the stairs. 'If you are going to fetch your aunt, it is not necessary,' he said. 'I asked Pillar to take a tea tray up to her and Goderich.'

'Oh! I shall say good night to him while I am here, then.'

They went together to the room, where Goderich and Emily had just interrupted a game of cards to take their tea. No air of romance hung about them.

In fact, Mrs Lipton looked weary, but when Jane and Nick entered, her eyes brightened.

'Has something happened belowstairs?' she asked eagerly.

'No, we are just having tea,' Jane said, wondering at her aunt's strange eagerness. 'I came to tell you, but I see you are having yours here. What did you think might have happened?'

'Why, nothing, to be sure.'

'We have been looking at all the things Mrs Huddleston bought in Brighton.'

'And discussing asses,' Nick added. Again that eager look seized Mrs Lipton's face. 'Four-legged ones,' he added, smiling.

'I have assembled a dandy herd of donkeys, Ronald,' Goderich said. 'I mean to send them to . . .' He frowned. 'They use them in Spain, you know.'

'Yes, but the war is over, Uncle.'

'I know it. We won. But that is why I bred them. For Wellington! That's it! My memory is improving, eh, Lily?'

'Much better,' Emily said.

'Are you going to waltz for me tonight?' Goderich asked the young couple.

'Not tonight, Lord Goderich,' Jane said firmly.

'Goderich has been telling me about your waltz,' Mrs Lipton said. She had thought he imagined it, and wondered now that Jane had not mentioned it to her.

Nick took Jane's fingers and smiled at her. 'Not tonight, unfortunately, Uncle. But you shall see us waltz at your New Year's party.'

'I am looking forward to it. Rogers has taken my evening suit down to be pressed.'

Jane twitched her hand away from Nick's grasp.

Why had he done that? This flirtatious behavior was quite improper in an engaged gentleman. He answered her scowl with a bold, teasing grin.

'I shall go downstairs now,' Jane said.

'Yes, we will leave you two now,' Nick added.

'There is no need for you to rush away,' she said to Nick.

'You must know how eager I am to return to our company.'

She could think of no sensible reply to this except a scold. As soon as they were out of the room, she delivered it.

'Don't think to engage me in any disparagement of your future in-laws, Nick. It is quite horrid of you to poke fun at them behind their backs.'

He assumed a mask of astonishment. 'Disparagement? Did I not say I was eager to rejoin them?'

'Yes, said it in that smart-alecky way. I know comparisons are odious, and you will not like to be compared to Willie, but he is behaving more properly than you, with regard to your company.'

'Meaning he is trying to beat my time with Aurelia?'

'Certainly not! That was not my meaning at all. I mean he tries to smooth out any little difficulties that arise between the two families, to change the subject when . . .'

He looked at her, with a slow smile stretching his lips. 'Do go on. I am all ears to learn a lesson from Willie.'

'You know perfectly well what I mean.'

'Yes, I am afraid I do. I must console myself that at least you did not suggest I take a leaf from Horace's book, and drown my woes in a bottle.'

'Why do you speak of woes? Surely these days before a man's wedding should be – are some of the happiest days of his life.'

'I, for one, can scarcely contain my joy. And now if you have nothing either sensible or interesting to say, let us go below.'

'No, you do not escape that easily, sir. Are you saying you are unhappy with your engagement?'

'That would be ungentlemanly.'

'So is trying to flirt with me behind Aurelia's back. I won't have it, Nick.'

He just smiled softly. 'It is hardly necessary for you to tell me you are not "that sort of girl," dear Jane. Your interest in my behavior is most gratifying. I feared it was only Pel you were determined to reform.'

'You are both incorrigible! I wash my hands of the pair of you.'

'Then may I take it the grand romance with Pel has floundered on the shoals of common sense?'

'There was never any romance to it, as you know very well. I leave the romance to you. And it is pretty clear you will make a botch of it, too, the way you are going about it.'

'I have not Willie's knack with the ladies. I don't see him holding your hand as he did when he first arrived. Another interrupted romance?'

'He is not gauche enough to do his courting in public.'

Nick gave her a sharp look. 'Meaning he is after you in private? Is that it?'

'Perhaps,' she said insouciantly, although it was not true.

'I thought you had more sense! As if making up to Pel were not bad enough, now you are letting that scoundrel of a Willie dangle after you.'

'It is none of your affair, Nick,' she said, in good humor at his jealousy.

'It ought to be someone's.'

When she just laughed, Nick realized she had been teasing him. He leaned against the banister, halfway down the grand staircase, with his arms crossed, as if settling in for a discussion. 'This love is a difficult business, is it not? It seems neither romance nor common sense by itself is enough. What can the answer be?'

'Celibacy,' she said, and continued on alone, while Nick stood looking after her with a bemused smile on his lips.

'That wasn't the answer I had in mind,' he called after her.

She refused to acknowledge his parting shot, but being only human, and in love, she did wonder what he meant.

She went and sat with Pel to take her tea, refusing to so much as look at Nick, and thinking of nothing else but him. The group made an early night of it. The Huddleston party was tired from shopping, and Lady Elizabeth was fagged from trying to entertain them. And on top of it all, the Townsends were due to arrive in a few days.

Before retiring, Nick went to the study and wrote a note to Lord Castlereagh about a posting in Paris. He was so eager to proceed with his romance that he sent it off with a footman that very night, with orders that he should await a reply, and ride *ventre à terre* back to Clareview the instant he had the answer. Unfortunately, Lord Castlereagh had gone home to Cray's Foot for the holiday, and did not receive the letter for a few days.

# Chapter Seventeen

*T*he few remaining days until the arrival of the Townsends passed in a flurry of activity for the hostess and a good deal of ennui for the guests. Marie said it was as well she and Horace were there to amuse 'Relia, for it was pretty clear the bridegroom had other things on his mind. This was no snide reference to Jane, but to his work on the estate. If he was not out with his agent, he was at a cattle auction, or at the bank, or in his study.

'You must certainly get him away from Clareview, 'Relia,' Marie advised. 'I had not thought Nick was such a demon for work. He was more attentive in London, before he was sure of winning you. When we get him back to London, you will see more of him. No one works in London. Horace goes for days at a time without darkening the door of his office, you must know. He is such a comfort to me. I always know just where he is.'

Jane was in a state of confusion. It was true Nick no longer behaved like a lover. She thought he should spend more time with his fiancée. He was usually with Aurelia in the evening at least, and appeared to be in good enough spirits, but there was some mystery, or mischief, in him that she could not quite under-stand. She could not help notice that his first ardor had cooled. His preference was for some activity that included others besides Aurelia and himself. As Aurelia disliked cards, they usually played some childish game with Pel or Willie and herself. She often looked up to find Nick's dark eyes studying her intently.

Twice he had followed her to the library, and engaged her in a longish conversation. Another time he had sought her out in Lizzie's private parlor where she was writing letters. That time, as well, he had remained chatting until she suggested he return to his fiancée, as his work left him so little time with Aurelia. There had been nothing lover-like in those few conversations. They had spoken of the days before Nick went to Spain, and of old friends. Once he had told her a little more about his experiences in Spain, but usually the tone had been more nostalgic than anything else. Nick's seeking her out so often was unsettling, the more so as it gave her so much pleasure.

On the day of the party, she had to go to the conservatory to speak to James about finding enough blooms to decorate the ballroom and arranging for the removal of the palms to the front hall. Nick had elected to remain at home that day. To prevent Mrs Huddleston from taking a pet, Jane chose to slip away while Nick was not around, lest he follow her again.

She had not been in the conservatory more than a minute when Nick appeared at the doorway. 'So this is where you are,' he said, coming forward.

'Were you looking for me?' she asked, trying to keep her tone natural. It was not easy when he smiled at her with that bright eager-ness glowing in his eyes. 'Or is it James you have come to see?'

He didn't answer the question, but held a palm frond aside and looked around the room. 'I like a conservatory in winter,' he said. 'It is so warm and moist.'

'Yes, it is pleasant.'

'Where is James?'

'I don't know. Perhaps he has gone out. He was going to cut some fresh mistletoe. The branches we cut are beginning to wilt. Some of the berries are falling.'

Nick took a step closer to her. Sensing danger, she stepped back, brushing against a lemon tree. 'Ouch!' she exclaimed as a thorn grazed her fingers.

Nick used it as an excuse to seize her hand and examine it. 'It is only a scratch,' she said, swiftly drawing her fingers back.

'I am tame, Jane. I don't bite,' he said, taking her hand again and gripping it firmly. 'You work too hard. You are always busy.'

'My biggest chore is finding something to do. It is you who is working too hard.' When she wiggled her fingers free, he gave a knowing grin.

'Work is good for the soul,' he said.

'Then yours must be in prime shape. You have been working almost too hard, for ... I mean, when your fiancée and her family are visiting.'

'There is a great deal to be done. Business before pleasure. As you will notice, I am at liberty today for any pleasure you care to suggest.'

'I thought you were here on business – looking for James.'

He gave a mischievous smile. 'Oh, is that what you thought?'

Looking around, she spotted a basket of freshly cut mistletoe on a table. 'I see James has already been out,' she said.

Nick went to the basket and held up a bough. 'I missed my kiss this year,' he said, looking at her in a quizzical manner.

'No, you didn't. I saw you kissing Aurelia under the kissing bough.'

'Did you, now? And you didn't rush forward to catch me while I was at your tender mercy?'

Jane was uneasy with his strange mood. There was an excitement in his eyes, an impatience that she could not account for, almost as if he were gloating over some secret. He had not been in this mood on the other occasions when he had sought her out.

'Why don't you take the mistletoe to Pillar and have him hang it for tonight?' she suggested, hoping to be rid of him.

'You are forgetting the tradition.'

'The tradition is that the family hang the evergreens. We have already done that.'

'I was referring to the tradition of the kissing bough.' He held the mistletoe bough over her head and leaned forward to place a quick kiss on her cheek.

Jane, realizing at the last moment what he was up to, turned her head sharply aside to avoid it. Instead, she brought her lips into contact with Nick's. The kiss had the effect of an electrical charge. A sharp surge of excitement coursed through her body, momentarily riveting her to the spot, while the kiss lingered sweetly on her lips. She shook herself back to reality and withdrew a few inches, staring at him silently. Some awful knowledge was born between them in the brief seconds of that self-conscious look.

Nick didn't speak. He just tossed the mistletoe back into the basket and drew her into his arms. And she let him. She went, like one in trance, hypnotized by the soft warmth of the tropical oasis around them that hardly seemed like real life at all, by the glitter of desire that had suddenly blazed in his eyes, and most of

182

all by an overwhelming realization that she felt that same need.

It was an unconscionable, unforgivable thing, to do. Nick was engaged, but she could no more stop herself than she could stop a flying bullet. It was as if some wild force had taken control of her mind and body. His lips firmed in demand as he crushed her against him in a ruthless, plundering embrace that left her breathless. She felt as if she were melting from the inside out from the heat that grew in her. She couldn't tell whether the awful guilt made the kiss better or worse, but at length it could no longer be ignored, and she pushed him away.

'Jane.' His voice throbbed a whispering need, then he reached out his arms to take her again.

'Stop it,' she gasped. 'Just stop it, Nick. How dare you – I have been feeling sorry for you. I come to think you and Miss Aurelia will do very well together.'

He leapt on her words like a dog on a bone. 'What does that mean?'

'You figure it out.'

'No, you tell me. Are you suggesting there is another man? Has she confided in you?' he asked hopefully. Surely that quick, eager question indicated hopefulness. He wanted to be rid of Aurelia!

'Certainly not. But I, for one, would not blame her if there were someone else, for she has not seen much of *you* all week. I hardly know which of you has behaved more badly.'

'Desperate times call for desperate measures.'

'Don't think to use *me* to execute whatever vile scheme you are hatching. It has nothing to do with me.'

'Ah, but there you are wrong, my sweet. It has everything to do with you.'

'I should have thought an officer and a gentleman would take the blame for his own mistakes.' On this curt insult she turned and fled from the conservatory. She went straight to her room and missed Sir William's announcement of his new appointment.

Willie's first reaction upon receiving the offer earlier that morning had been to assume the letter had gone to the wrong person. He took it to Nick.

'I have received a most bizarre missive from Lord Castlereagh asking if I would consider a posting to Paris to act in a liaison capacity between Wellington's Paris office and the Department of Foreign Affairs in London. What can it mean?' he asked in confusion.

Nick glanced briefly at the letter and smiled blandly. 'Why, it looks as if you have friends in high places, Willie. Congratulations. This sounds like a posting much to your advantage. Paris is gay at this time. The half of London society will be there. And the duties, you know, will not be onerous. Attending official parties, chaperoning a few dignitaries about town, and going often to London to report to Castlereagh.'

'It sounds like a dream, but how . . . ?' A smile moved his lips. 'You!'

'A pity Castlereagh had not seen fit to offer the post to me, as Aurelia is so eager to visit Paris. I, alas, will be much too busy here.'

Willie understood him perfectly. 'But the engagement has been announced,' he said.

'So was the Duke of Halford and Miss Rennet's, but no wedding occurred. The path of true love, as we are all tired of knowing, never did run smooth. Of course, a gentleman cannot call off. That is the privilege of the bride-to-be.'

'Marie will never let her do it.'

'Will she not? I will not even be a sir when Uncle marries Mrs Lipton. Your bride, on the other hand, will be Lady Winston.'

'Goderich marry! You must be—' He stopped, chuckled, and said, 'You, sir, are the wiliest gentleman in the parish.' He bowed in acknowledgment of the fact. 'I cede the crown to your superior talents, cousin. Another announcement of a wedding that will not take place. When will the announcement be made?'

'At the New Year's party, I think, but you will want to inform our guests of your great fortune before that time – as soon as you have written to Castlereagh accepting the post, I should think. You must not forget that important detail.' He stood up and offered Willie the seat at the desk.

Willie reached for the pen. 'My hand is trembling,' he said. 'Do you know, this will be the first job I have ever had?'

'You mustn't believe everything you hear. An old dog can learn new tricks.'

'Aye, if the reward is high enough. I just want you to know, Nick – I do care for her, you know. This is not just cream-pot love.'

'I know you do, Willie. You must care for her even more than you know, to have withstood such prolonged bouts of shopping without a single complaint.'

'I realize she is a widgeon, and as common as Judy O'Grady, but – dash it, I like her. She suits me. And this post will just suit her family. A touch of class, you know. That is my main attraction.'

'I wouldn't say that, Willie. Not to disparage your elegant way, but you are a good-natured fellow. The FO will take care of your moving expenses, but if you need a little something to be going on with – I thought a wedding gift . . .'

'Fifty pounds should cover it.'

'Optimist!' Nick said, laughing, and wrote him a check for twice that sum.

After this conversation, Nick went in search of Jane in the conservatory, and Willie went to the saloon to make his own announcement.

'Well, upon my word!' Marie exclaimed when she heard the wonderful news. 'How did this happen? Who do you know in the government, Willie? I wager it was the Prince Regent who arranged it. You are hand in glove with him.'

'It could have been Lord Byron,' Aurelia suggested. 'I told you, Marie, Willie knows everyone.'

'Now, there we are, Horace,' Marie said to her husband. 'We will not need 'Relia's connections to get into society in Paris after all. Willie will pave our way.'

'Oh, Willie, you cannot mean you are leaving England!' Aurelia exclaimed.

'Duty calls,' Willie said, matching her woe. 'The hardest thing will be leaving my dear, dear friends behind.'

'We won't be a week behind you,' Marie assured him. 'And Nick has promised to take 'Relia over in the spring.'

Willie picked up Aurelia's silken fan and fingered it sadly. 'What a long winter it will be,' he sighed.

'I think it is horrid of you to leave me!' Aurelia said, and ran, sobbing, from the room.

It was Jane's intention to stay away from Nick as much as possible, or at least not to be alone with him again. When she had recovered from her experience in the conservatory, she was told Willie's news, and congratulated him. There was no sign of Nick, but to be safe, she sent a footman to the conservatory for the flowers and helped arrange them, in company with Mrs Lipton. At luncheon she did not once look within a right angle of the head of the table. No one noticed, as the talk was all of Willie's new position.

The next excitement at Clareview was the arrival of Edward Townsend and his wife at four o'clock that same afternoon. It was clear at a glance where Marie got her disposition, and both ladies their looks. At fifty years, Mrs Townsend still wore the fading traces of beauty, along with a very smart pelisse and bonnet. Mr Townsend had the truculent air of the self-made man who knows he is more capable (and richer) than his so-called betters. He was short and red-faced, with the sort of stomach that results from a prolonged ingestion of beefsteak and ale.

He went about the saloon, pumping hands and slapping backs and making himself at home.

'So this is 'Relia's future home. So out-of-the-way, I thought we would never find it. All that land along the road belongs to you, does it, Colonel?'

'The last few miles of it are part of my uncle's estate,' Nick replied.

'Seems a shame for it to be sitting idle.'

'It is pasture for the cows, and of course, some barley and wheat.'

'You ought to put up some houses there.' He looked around the room. Darkness had fallen early on the last day of December. 'Or build a new one for yourself and 'Relia, eh? But then, Marie tells me these old heaps are all the rage. A bit old for my taste, dark and drafty, too.' He cast a sharp, appraising glance around the room. 'You ought to put in a new Rumford grate. If you threw out a couple of bow windows, you would have a better view. Mind you, there is not much to see save grass and trees. We threw out one in Ellie's new house. She lives in that window, watching the people passing by.' His eyes descended to the floor, where the one new carpet stood out in sharp relief to the older one below it. 'I see you are beginning to spruce the place up,' he said. 'Still, it is not a bad place. Not bad at all.' His eyes strayed again to the park, where so much land was unplanted. 'I see potential here.'

It was not until this verdict was delivered that Lady Elizabeth could get around to making introductions, and Aurelia to boasting of having met the Prince of Wales.

'He knew of me, did he?' Townsend asked, pleased with his fame. 'I shall get you to hit him up for a royal warrant for my Oldham Ale after the marriage, 'Relia. "Suppliers to the Prince of Wales" on the label would add I don't know how many gallons per annum. What price do you figure he asks for an endorsement, Colonel?'

Nick was unable to oblige him with a figure. It was Willie who was aware of such matters. 'You must apply to the lord chamberlain. Hennessey paid a thousand for his royal warrant for mustard. Under the table, of course. In theory, the royal warrant is earned by the quality of the product.'

'I will offer him two thousand. Edward Townsend does not go, cap in hand, to anyone.'

During this interval and the serving of a welcoming glass of wine, servants in a steady stream moved from the front door to the stairway, carrying all manner of luggage, and creating a wicked draft.

'P'raps they ought to have used the back door for that,' Marie said uncertainly.

'I like to keep an eye on my employees,' Townsend said, and

indeed did keep a sharp eye on them as they labored under the weight of trunks and boxes. 'Turn your back on them for a minute and they are sitting on their thumbs. Here, Jack! Mind you don't bump against that table. That is a brand-new trunk you are carrying.'

'And the table is priceless,' Lizzie added.

It was Marie who made the announcement of Willie's new posting.

'You never mean it! Paree?' Mrs Townsend exclaimed. 'You will be able to call on 'Relia and Nick, Sir William.'

'We will not be going to Paris until the spring, Mama,' Aurelia said, and tossed her curls at Nick to show her displeasure.

Mr Townsend spoke in his carrying voice, drowning out whatever shock or grief the ladies might have indulged in at this tragic news.

'My congrats to you, Sir William. I never thought you had it in you. Here I have been taking you for a shiftless sort of fellow, from what Marie tells me. Ran through your own inheritance, I think?'

'For my sins,' Willie admitted, 'but I have turned over a new leaf, Mr Townsend.'

'Never too late to mend. I always believe in giving a fellow a second chance.'

Jane, Lady Elizabeth, Mrs Lipton, Pelham, and Nick just sat and listened, for it was impossible to speak with so many Townsends all talking at once. The Townsend ladies kept up their own undercurrent of chatter while Mr Townsend held the floor. Odd scraps of conversation were overheard amidst the din of 'tied houses' and 'one hundred thousand gallons.' 'Smartest bonnet – Brighton, of course – a new fur muff –' Eventually it was time to go abovestairs and prepare for the evening.

In the general melee, Jane found herself walking upstairs with Nick. Her head was swimming from nearly two hours of incessant shouting and chatter, without anything of the least importance having been said.

'Cat got your tongue?' he asked.

She essayed a wan smile. 'Your future in-laws are very . . . gregarious,' she said.

'That is strange. I scarcely heard them utter a word.'

She stared in confusion. 'Your hearing must be impaired from the war.'

'Yes, my hearing, too,' he said, and smiled nonchalantly.

They parted at the head of the stairs. Mrs Lipton said, while they were dressing, 'Lizzie has decided to remove to the Dower House if Nick marries her.'

'*If?* Surely it is too late to speak of *if.*'

Too late. The awful words were with her as she dressed. She wished she had not let Nick kiss her in the conservatory. Now she knew what she was missing. Yet she could not be so very sorry. At least she had had one small taste of the true glory of love.

# Chapter Eighteen

No grass grew under Edward Townsend's feet. While ostensibly abovestairs preparing for dinner, he had taken a quick self-guided tour of Clareview. He had been born and raised in a small cottage in Manchester. When he made his fortune, he built himself the grandest mansion his imagination and money could contrive, but he began to see that it was not enough. A man needed the stretching acres, the picture gallery with old pictures, and the armaments room full of rusty arms that had been around before Gaul was divided into three, before he had really arrived.

He had been told it was all the crack to have aristocratic connections, and while it had been his experience in the past that he could buy whatever he wanted, he began to sense that not all things could be purchased. He had encountered Pillar during the course of his self-appointed tour. Pillar had spoken of Goderiches going back for centuries, of wars he had never heard of, in which Goderiches defended monarchs who were also unknown by name to him. 'We are strong on tradition at Clareview,' he said at one point.

A man could not buy tradition, but by God, he could rub up against it to remove the rough edges of commerce if his daughter was a genuine lady. Hunting, for instance, was a sport that had always attracted him. It would be fine to be darting through a field in a red jacket, mounted on a prime bit o' blood, rattling after Reynard. He envisaged himself as Master of Hounds, leading the pack. And it was little 'Relia who would introduce him to this new style of life that stretched enticingly before him.

While he discussed these matters with Mrs Townsend, Jane Ramsey dressed in her dark green velvet grown for dinner and the evening. She had not that luxurious surfeit of gowns possessed by the Townsends. Nick was looking out for her, and when he espied her descending the staircase, with her coppery curls sitting like a crown on her head, he felt a wrenching inside. What if his plan didn't work? What if he had to go through with this wedding with Aurelia? What if Aurelia begged off, and Jane still refused to have him? He had disgusted her by his behavior that morning. He would be at pains to act the role of gentleman tonight.

As soon as he saw Jane, he nipped back into the saloon and was found seated next to his fiancée when Jane entered the saloon. Her eyes flew directly to him. He sensed it without turning to see, as if by some extrasensory power. The only empty seat in the group was next to Mr Townsend, and she took it, to have her poor ears bombarded by tales of acquisitions of tied houses, and the price of hops.

'I have been looking into buying my own hop farm,' he said. 'But after seeing all the colonel's acres sitting next door to idle, growing corn, I see no reason why I should not hire the land from my son-in-law. Are there any hops grown hereabouts, Miss . . . or is it Mrs?'

'Miss Ramsey.'

'Well, what about it?'

'There is a hop farm five miles down the road.'

'I thought as much! The location will be convenient when I open my Kent brewery.'

She was reprieved by the announcement of dinner. Pel came to accompany her to the table.

'I hope my mouth still knows how to open. I have not been able to speak since this batch of yahoos landed in,' he grumbled.

He had no difficulty getting it open to eat once dinner was on the table. The talk was a solo performance by Edward Townsend. The colonel sat at the head of the table, but there was no doubt as to who ruled the roast. Townsend only interrupted his talk to shovel forkfuls of roast beef and potatoes into his mouth. With no conversational duties, Jane was free to observe her companions. She found it distinctly strange that everyone appeared so contented. Mr Townsend's behavior was nothing new to his own family, of course, but it was odd that Lady Elizabeth and Nick showed no dismay at his *farouche* behavior.

She could only conclude that her scold to Nick had borne results, and he was on his best behavior. Being unable to speak to Aurelia, Nick smiled often in her direction, and kept offering her things from the table. She hardly ate a bite. Halfway through the meal she put down her fork and picked up her fan, to toy with it while sulking in Willie's direction.

After dinner, the ladies moved gratefully to the saloon, to give their ears a rest. Before long, the gentlemen joined them, and soon the other guests for the rout began to arrive. Although it was not a formal ball, Aurelia and Nick opened the dancing.

'I would have liked to see the colonel in his regimentals,'

Townsend said to the little group around him, 'but he is a fine figure of a lad, even in a black jacket. I will be happy to have him as a son-in-law.'

Jane thought Nick might have stood up once with her without causing any scandal, but he didn't ask her. He stood up with Marie Huddleston and several of the neighbors, but not with her. The dancing continued unabated until eleven-thirty, at which time the music stopped and Lord Goderich was led into the room, propped up on one side by Nick and on the other by Willie. His black evening suit had been pressed to within an inch of its life. At his throat, a diamond as big as a cherry sparkled in his white cravat. His hair was brushed and he had had a fresh shave for the occasion. The neighbors surged forward to wish him well and congratulate him on being mobile again.

'Here is the little lady who is responsible for it,' Goderich said, taking Mrs Lipton's hand. Mrs Lipton gave a simpering smile, so unlike her usual sensible behavior. 'Will you tell them, my dear, or shall I?' he asked archly.

'Let Nick make the announcement,' Mrs Lipton said.

Nick went to the platform that had been erected for the orchestra, to make the formal announcement.

'It gives me great pleasure to announce that Mrs Lipton has accepted my uncle's offer of marriage,' he said.

A flurry of excitement ensued, drowning out any other words he might have planned to add. The neighbours, after they had digested their shock, clapped weakly. Jane stared at her aunt in disbelief. Aunt Emily marrying Goderich? It was impossible!

'Bit of a shocker,' Pel said, pulling at his ear. 'Still, no denying the old gaffer is improving every day.'

The Townsends were less tentative in their disapproval. 'Mad as a hatter!' Marie scolded.

'It is no odds,' Townsend said, after a good scrutiny of Goderich. 'He will be pushing up daisies in no time. 'Relia will still be a countess.'

'You never can tell,' his good wife cautioned. 'It only takes one time. And she, you know, is not all that old. If she has a son ...'

'Rubbish! The old boy is inches from the grave. You don't throw over an earl for that. I have plans for Clareview.'

His wife and daughter exchanged a meaningful look. 'I'll speak to 'Relia,' Marie said, and the two of them went in search of her.

It was Marie who did the talking. 'I knew it!' she said. 'I warned Nick, but he wouldn't listen to me.'

'I think it's sweet,' Aurelia said.

'Simpleton! What if Nick is diddled out of his inheritance? He has scarcely a feather to fly with of his own. Only seven hundred acres, and a little house with thirty rooms. And he hasn't the wits to make use of his connections. Letting Willie waltz off to Paris on a posting that should, by rights, be his. He knows you are dying to go to Paree. I would not sit still for it if I were you, 'Relia. Upon my word, I would not.'

'She has her heart set on a wedding,' Mrs Townsend said, looking across the room at Nick in an appraising way. 'We have spent over a hundred pounds on the gown.'

'It need not be wasted,' Marie said, her eyes turning to Willie, who came sidling forward.

'This is a bit of a shocker for you,' he said. 'I had no idea this was in the wind.'

'Then you are a bigger fool than I took you for,' Marie said, in her anger. 'I warned Nick—'

'He can be headstrong,' Willie said.

'He can be a demmed fool, but that is no need for us to be.'

Nick watched the group from his uncle's side. After Goderich and Mrs Lipton were installed in chairs at the edge of the room to watch the dancing, he joined the Townsend ladies, who greeted him with a noticeable chill.

At midnight the wassailers came around with their bowls trimmed in evergreen garlands and sang in the New Year.

'Here's to our horse and to his right ear,
God send our master a happy New Year;
A happy New Year as e'er he did see,
With my wassailing bowl I drink to thee!'

After they had left, champagne was served and the New Year greeted with the old traditional songs, sung in a circle. Goderich and Mrs Lipton were given special chairs in the middle of the circle. Goderich smiled and tapped time with his toe, and while he didn't join in the singing, it was obvious that he enjoyed hearing it.

Jane stood across the circle from Nick. She had thought that if anything would bring this wedding to a halt, the shocking announcement of Goderich's marriage might do it. She had a fair notion it was the likelihood of Nick's inheriting the title that was his main attraction to the Townsends.

It was odd, too, that Nick was taking it so well. Surely he ought to be feeling just a little put out at this engagement. But he obviously wasn't. He looked as happy as he had the evening he arrived with his fiancée on his arm, just over a week ago. Was it the possibility of losing out on Clareview that had finally resigned him to marrying his heiress? He was being more attentive to Aurelia than usual, and hardly glanced at herself at all. That easily he had forgotten those magical moments in the conservatory. It was all very confusing.

A late supper was served after the champagne and singing. Goderich was too fagged to join in; he was escorted upstairs, but Mrs Lipton remained. Jane sat with her and Pelham, trying to join in the merriment, but her heart wasn't in it. When Nick suggested more dancing after supper, she excused herself and went upstairs with her Aunt Emily.

'I had no idea you and Goderich were so close,' Jane said.

'I doubt anything will come of it, Jane. He took the notion he wanted to become engaged, and I went along to keep him happy. It is unlikely I will ever be removing to Clareview, if that is what distresses you.'

'I am not particularly distressed, just surprised. Shocked, in fact.'

'You weren't the only one! Did you see the neighbors stare! Who did take it very well is Mr Townsend. I hope – feared he might take a pet, but it is no such a thing. I heard him speaking to Nick just before we left. He was saying something about raising hops here at Clareview, and inquiring about the local hunt. It seems the wedding will take place after all.'

Jane listened and said, 'Was that what you hoped to accomplish by this engagement? To get Aurelia to beg off?'

'We had to do something, but it didn't work. It seems Nick is stuck with her. Well, he has made his bed, and now he must lie in it. I'm sorry, Jane.' She gave Jane's fingers a consoling squeeze.

Jane was already inured to the fact that she had lost Nick. She had only one question to ask. 'Was your engagement to Goderich Nick's idea?'

'I hope you don't think it was mine! I stood out against it as long as I could, but when I realized how very much he wanted out of this marriage, I had to give in. I fear there is no hope of Aurelia calling off. Townsend has decided he wants to grow hops here at Clareview, and won't let her.'

That was Jane's little consolation. Nick didn't want to marry Aurelia. She thought he wanted to marry her. Why could he not have delayed his offer to Aurelia until he had come home for Christmas? Too late now . . .

# Chapter Nineteen

'Leave it until morning, Pillar,' Nick said.

The neighbors had gone home, the guests who were staying at Clareview had gone to bed, and most of the party debris had been cleared away. Nick just wanted to sit alone in front of the grate and brood.

The announcement of Goderich's marriage had been his last hope. Refusing to get married at St. George's Church and honeymoon in Paris hadn't done it. Making Willie as eligible as time allowed hadn't done it. The devil of it was that he knew Aurelia didn't want to marry him any more than he wanted to marry her. Townsend, of course, was the crux of it. Nick had observed from a little distance the hurried discussions between the Townsends when Goderich's marriage was announced. He had seen Aurelia's sulks and the dark looks Marie shot in his direction – and he had seen Edward Townsend shake his head adamantly.

Townsend had taken the notion that he wanted to raise hops at Clareview. He spoke of "snapping up" another few thousand acres nearby. Nick had said, without being asked, that he had no intention of running a brewery.

'I should say not, lad! You are too noble a specimen to stick behind a desk. We can put you to better use.'

Put him to use, as if he were one of those donkeys in the barn, eating its head off. A long future of life with the Townsend ménage paraded before his eyes. He and Horace, slipping off for a bottle in the library. Oh God! He wished he were back in Spain. And worst of all was losing Jane. Happiness dangled an inch before him, like a shimmering mirage, unattainable. He extinguished all the lamps and sat in the dark, gazing into the grate, seeing her flaming hair dancing in the ever-changing pattern of the fire, and her eyes staring at him accusingly.

For a long time he sat, while the level of wine in the bottle beside him lowered. Finally he dozed off. When he awoke, the fire had dwindled to embers that glowed through the white ash. By their dim light, he drew out his watch and read the hour. Four o'clock. He wondered what had awoken him. The chiming of the long-case clock, perhaps. He rose, yawned, and stretched. Wide awake now, he decided he wanted a drink of brandy, to induce sleep, for he knew it would be a long, hard night once he was in his bed. He would take the decanter from the dining room upstairs with him.

From the dining room, he heard a whispering sound, followed by a snicker of laughter. It came from the grand staircase. Who could it be? Then a lower voice spoke softly – a man's voice. The servants sneaking downstairs to snitch a bottle of wine? He didn't mind that, but if one of the footmen was carrying on an illicit romance, he had best give him a lecture. 'Marry the wench if you love her, fool!' he would say.

He trod softly along the hallway toward the staircase as two dark forms slipped into the Gold Saloon. That was really too encroaching! If the servants were using the best saloon for clandestine romance, he would turn them off. There, lined in a ray of moonlight and the soft glow from the grate, he discerned the tall, bulky form of a man dressed in a greatcoat. Willie! Now, what the devil . . .

He looked at the woman, recognized the high poke bonnet of his fiancée, and froze to the spot. She was wearing a pelisse, and carrying a bandbox. It couldn't be – surely it was not an elopement! As he watched, with his heart pounding in joyful hope, Aurelia went forward and placed a note on the mantel of the fireplace.

'I don't know what Papa will say, Willie,' she said.

'Your papa is a realist. What can he say, when the deed is done?'

'Marie will calm him down. She has promised to have my gowns sent to Paree. Oh, Willie, I feel so sorry for poor Nick. His heart will be broken.'

'Hearts mend, my darling. All's fair in love and war. Come, the carriage is waiting. I told my groom to have it at the door at four on the dot.'

He took her hand to lead her into the hallway and out the door, while Nick stood with a smile stretching from ear to ear. He could not suppress his joy. One victorious peal of laughter rang out. He wanted to run upstairs to awaken Jane and tell her the news. As this was ineligible, he went to the mantel and picked up the note. He read it by the dying embers of the grate. 'Dear Nick: Willie and I are going to London to be married tomorrow by special license as he has to leave so soon for Paris.'

Not Gretna Green? He was surprised, but delighted that no possibility of chasing after them was necessary. They would be in

London by daybreak, and hopefully married before anyone could reach them. 'I am sorry, but I love him too much to let him leave. I hope you will try to understand. Regards, Aurelia Townsend. P.S. We will be pleased if you would visit us sometime in Paris.'

He replaced the note and just sat in the chair, smiling and uttering silent thanks to whatever kind deity had heard his prayer and answered it.

Abovestairs, Jane was in her bed, but she was not asleep. She had lain in the darkness with dry eyes, thinking of the future as she stared across the room at the rectangle of lighter gray against the darker wall, formed by moonlight seeping through the window curtains. After what had happened in the conservatory, she had given up all thought of marrying Pelham. He had not pursued his first tentative mention of marriage, and she was glad of it. She would probably become a spinster, like Lady Elizabeth.

After hours of futile repining, she was just dozing off to sleep when she heard muffled footfalls in the hallway, and the surreptitious opening of a doorway close by. Aurelia's room, was it? She rose up quietly from her bed and went to the door to listen. Perhaps Aurelia was ill. She opened her own door a crack and saw Mrs Huddleston going into the room. If Aurelia was ill, her sister would tend to her. Jane went back to bed. Slight rustling sounds continued to come from Aurelia's room, and an occasional soft giggle. The sisters enjoying a bit of gossip. Very likely they could not sleep after the party either. It must be nice to have a sister . . .

It was some time later when she heard a different sound, coming from beyond her window. What could it be at this hour? She went and opened her curtains. A carriage and team of four were being driven out of the stable. It was difficult to tell whose carriage. In the shadows, they all looked alike. But who could be leaving in the middle of the night? The team of four suggested a long journey. Curiosity made sleep impossible. She returned to listen at the door, and was just in time to hear Aurelia's door open.

'Well, I am off, Marie. Wish me well,' Aurelia said.

She was off? Off to where?

'You are doing the right thing, my dear. An elopement – so romantic. I shall talk Papa down from the boughs, never fear. Mama is on our side, so all is well. Off you go, now.'

An elopement! Jane remembered that Nick had suggested it, but she never imagined Aurelia would consider such a thing, when St. George's was already booked and that expensive wedding gown under construction. How had he talked her into it? And why? Was he afraid Townsend would not let him marry Aurelia, after Goderich's engagement? Impetuous fool!

The tears that had refused to come earlier came now in abundance. She threw herself on her bed and had a good cry. When it was all over, she put on her dressing gown and went downstairs to see if they had at least left a note. Her hope – or fear – was that Nick would have left a special note for her, and she did not want to have to explain that to anyone.

She crept quietly down the stairs and along the marble hallway to the Gold Saloon. From the doorway she discerned the white note propped against a pair of brass candlesticks. There seemed to be only the one note. She hastened forward. It was not until she was nearly there that she saw the dark form in the chair and uttered an instinctive yelp of shock.

'Oh! Who is it? Mr Huddleston?' She could think of no one

else who might behave so oddly. She assumed he was drunk, as usual.

The head turned, and she saw Nick, smiling at her.

'Nick! But you – Aurelia – I thought—' She looked around for Aurelia, but they were obviously alone. 'Where is she?'

'On route to London to marry Willie.'

'Willie!' she said, on a trembling breath of rising euphoria. 'I thought *you* were eloping!' She was weak with relief. The awful nightmare was over. She wanted to pitch herself into his arms and hang on to him for dear life.

Nick rose and gazed at her dear familiar face, with a tousle of curls falling to her shoulders. She looked, at that moment, like the girl he had foolishly left behind when he went off to Spain. He just gazed, storing up this treasured moment in the bank of memory. Her wobbly smile told him all he needed to know. Then he took her hand and drew her to his side.

'No, it is the tradition for the Morgans to marry at St. Peter's church, in Amberley. It is also the tradition for us to make a love match.'

'Then you don't mind that she's marrying Willie?'

'Mind? My dear girl, I have moved heaven and bent earth to bring this match off.'

'*You* got Willie the post in Paris?'

'*Mea culpa.* I also catapulted Uncle into an engagement he scarcely comprehends, to say nothing of Mrs Lipton, who was obliging in the extreme. I think you know why.'

She tilted her head to look up at him, but didn't speak. The moment was too precious to require words.

'God, I was such a fool. Rushing into a proposal to a girl I scarcely knew. I only knew that I wanted to marry and settle down. Aurelia was there – the prettiest girl I had met. Before I knew what I was about, I found myself shackled. Or as close to it as made no difference. Can you ever forgive me?'

'Oh, Nick!'

'I shall take that for a yes. Now for the big one. Darling, I love you so much, I . . .'

Words failed him. He drew her into his arms for a long, sweet embrace by the fading embers, whispering all the love he had had to suppress for so long. Jane felt not only the thunderbolt of love, but the flashing lightning of desire as passion mounted, and he crushed her against him as if he would never let her go. For an hour they sat together, talking about their close escape, and the future.

After such a late night, they did not come downstairs until eleven the next morning. Aurelia's note had been found and read, the elopement discussed, and its advantages and disadvantages thoroughly gone into.

'It need not hamper me from picking up a thousand or so acres hereabouts for my hops,' Townsend decided. 'I'll throw a mansion up on a few acres for 'Relia and Willie, for when he is in England. With his connections, we will fit into country society with no trouble.'

''Relia will still be called a lady,' Marie pointed out. 'Lady Winston.'

'Willie will be a real lord in no time,' Townsend decided. 'That lad knows his way around. A bosom bow of the prince.'

'It is a pity about the wedding,' Mrs Townsend said, thinking of all the planning that had gone into it.

'She can wear the gown when she is presented at court,' Marie pointed out.

The first meeting with the jilted bridegroom could not be anything but awkward. Regrets were expressed and forgiveness granted. Before noon, Townsend was drawing out his heavy turnip watch and saying that they had best be off.

'We'll stop at Tupper's Tavern in Gatwick for a spot of luncheon,' he said to no one in particular. 'I am thinking of adding it to my chain of tied houses. With luck, we will lay our heads on our own pillows tonight, and be there to give Lady Winston a little wedding party before she leaves for Paris. No reason the poor girl should be diddled out of a wedding party entirely.'

'You can have 'Relia's carpet and lamps and vase sent to my place, in Grosvenor Square,' Marie informed Lady Elizabeth.

'I will be very happy to,' Lady Elizabeth replied promptly.

Marie was impressed with her easy victory. There was quality for you, say what you would. She had expected to have to haggle for the goods.

The trunks were brought down and loaded on the two carriages. The farewells were so cordial, one would almost think Aurelia had come to Clareview for no other reason than to elope with Sir William.

When Mrs Lipton went abovestairs for a hand of all fours with her fiancé, she was not too disconcerted to discover he had forgotten their engagement. Everyone else soon forgot it, too. They had a different engagement to conjure with. Amberley thought the colonel had chosen well. The Townsends were well enough in small doses, but they could not like to think of them spoiling all the parties at Clareview with their overweening ways.

'I shall toddle along to have a word with George,' Pelham said. 'I believe he is having some sort of service at St. Peter's for New

Year's Day. I will tell him to get practicing up the wedding service for you two.'

'Won't you do it for us, Pel?' Jane asked. 'You have practiced it for days. You must know it by now.'

'Daresay I could do it, for you. I mean to say, you can always prompt me if I go astray, Jane. You know it better than I do.'

Nick could not like to think of his wedding being turned into a farce by Pel. 'I was hoping you would be my best man, Pel,' he said.

'Would I have to memorize anything?'

'Just carry the ring, and give it to me to put on Jane's finger.'

'Daresay I could manage that. Consider it done.' They saw Pel off, then went back into the house, to see the servants removing the festive boughs from the saloon.

'Come with me,' Nick said, leading Jane to the ballroom.

The kissing bough still hung in the archway. He placed her under it, saying, 'I have wanted to do this ever since I saw Pel kissing you. That was when I first began to realize my ghastly mistake.'

'What a slow top you are. I realized it long before that.'

'But you didn't do anything about it, wretch.'

'What could I have done?'

'This,' he said, and kissed her fiercely.

*Also by Joan Smith*
*and soon to be published:*

# DAMSEL IN DISTRESS

Lady Caroline attracted trouble like moths to a flame!

Her romantic antics provided society with a good many minor scandals – which didn't stop the incomparable Caro from catching the eye of Lord Dolmain, a dashing widower.

But as was customary with Caro, trouble intruded before romance could. Dolmain accused her of stealing a diamond necklace worn by his young daughter at her debut.

Though the charge was soon retracted, his lordship had practically destroyed Caroline's reputation. The only way to redeem herself was to find the true thief. But when murder enters the scene, Caro and Dolmain discover that two heads – and two hearts – are better than one!